Anne Marsh writes
paranormal romanc
always enjoy one m
writing romance aft
as a technical writer
ever-afters trumped
Northern California with her family and six cats.

INKED

ANNE MARSH

MILLS & BOON

First Published in Great Britain 2018
by Mills & Boon, an imprint of HarperCollins*Publishers*
1 London Bridge Street, London, SE1 9GF

© 2018 Anne Marsh

ISBN: 978-0-263-93215-7

MIX
Paper from
responsible sources
FSC **FSC™ C007454**
www.fsc.org

This book is produced from independently certified FSC™ paper
to ensure responsible forest management.
For more information visit www.harpercollins.co.uk/green.

Printed and bound in Spain
by CPI, Barcelona

For Jimmy the Cake Guy.

Clearly, the best guys bake, make cupcake
deliveries, and look out for the women in their
dorms and their lives.

Thank you!

CHAPTER ONE

Vik

BEFORE I TOUCH even so much as an inch of sweet, creamy skin I know I want to spank her, mark her. Make her mine. Take her heart-shaped ass and all the softness she's hiding from me. Doesn't hurt that she's wearing plain white cotton panties, the kind designed to cover up rather than to showcase but that instead makes a man like me think about turning good girls bad. She's tucked the waistband down to give me more room to work. Thoughtful as fuck, right? I can't stop looking at the tattoo chair where she's spread out, waiting for me to ink her. I'll be her first because nothing but virgin skin meets my greedy eye.

And here I'd thought tonight would be boring.

Located on a busy if seedy street in East Las Vegas, the tattoo parlor I run when I'm not taking care of Hard Rider business specializes in flash tattoos for the impulsive crowd. Ink Me fronts the sidewalk and passersby can look through our windows and watch whatever ink's in progress. Maybe my new client doesn't care if she gives lookie-loos a show. Maybe she loves the thrill. I won't judge. Christ knows, my list of guilty pleasures reads like an encyclopedia of vice. Won't make excuses or apologize, either. I know what I like and I make sure I get it. I'm a hedonist, not a fucking saint, and inking this pretty bitch is the much-needed cherry on today's shit sundae.

People like company when they dive into the deep end of the pool of sin and debauchery and virgin ass's blonde companion looks like an expert. The teeny black cocktail dress, mile-high heels and red leather choker scream fun. The hair flat-ironed into an im-maculate curtain adds a note of sophistication that in no way matches the grit of East Las Vegas. Someone who pays attention to the wrapping paper will take even more care with the contents. Bet she waxes or goes full Brazilian with one of those clit piercings I love to roll around my tongue. Usually, Blondie would be my favorite kind of present and I'd be half-way to unwrapping her using that goddamned choker as a leash, but tonight the gorgeous ass in my chair trumps all.

"Ladies. What can I do for you?" I nod at the blonde, a wave of strawberry and tequila hitting me hard. Hope to fuck the woman in my chair is more sober. Not good to ink anyone with more alcohol than blood in her veins.

"Harper wants a tattoo," Blondie announces.

What kind of name is Harper? It sounds uptight and tidy, way too organized for the lush pair of thighs hugging my chair even if it fits the clothes. The white cotton blouse folded up her back matches the no-nonsense panties...and is that a *business* skirt unbuttoned and unzipped to give me access? When you've banged as many women as I have, you learn a thing or two about clothes, and Dolce & Gabbana is expensive shit. Ups the odds of her not being underage, though. As long as she's not a lawyer or a judge in the daylight hours, we're good.

Or bad. Lady's choice.

The shirt, panties and skirt might come from the Good Girl closet, but her shoes are pure sex. The black suede laces up the front, showcasing the cutest toes. I see her feet all tied up with a fucking bow and I start thinking about getting some rope on the rest of her body and showing her just how good a little kink can feel.

You got to admire a woman who can dress for success from the ankles up and then make a guy come on the spot when she flashes her feet at him. From the length of her legs, she's tall—and the heels give her another four inches. I'm a big bastard, but she'll come up past my shoulder no problem. Not too skinny, either, thank fuck. She's generous in all the right places, not some fragile flower that can't take a hard pounding.

"Start on her ass and work your way up," Blondie orders.

Gladly.

Been doing that my whole life. Grew up rough, just me and my old man. He rode for a local club, giving me a dozen honorary uncles who had my back

and kicked the shit out of me whenever I needed it.
First beer at twelve, first woman at fifteen and first
bike at sixteen. Since I'd been a stupid shit, I'd barely
made it out of high school, too busy enjoying the
open road and free pussy to think long-term. A few
years in the US Navy fixed that. Wasn't cut out to
be a career soldier but I picked up some things from
Uncle Sam's crew—discipline, training, a love of ink
and the ability to cut loose when onshore. The life of
the fiesta, that's me. I'd boozed and cruised my way
around a dozen different ports of call and I'd left my
mark on them all.

Party never ended.

My old man didn't like my constant fiesta, but his
right to give me shit ended the day I turned eighteen
and signed my life over at the local recruiting station.
When I'd come home at twenty-one, we'd shared a
beer and awkward small talk. Wasn't that my old
man looked smaller and older, just…less big. Not sure
where my genes came from but my club brothers call
me the Viking for more than one reason. Not only do
I fight like a berserker, but I look like one, too. My
pretty face is just the party favor on a package of le-
thal. Ladies, you've been warned.

The beauty in my chair shifts impatiently. "Are
we starting?"

I jerk my eyes up to Beauty's head. Gotta stop staring at her ass. She has dark hair, a glossy brown so
dark it's almost black as it spills from the crown of
her head in a long, sleek ponytail. Christ, it's like she
looked inside my head and picked out all my favor-

ite fantasies. If we were alone, I'd be fisting that soft length as I pounded into her from behind.

I need my sex dirty and rough. *Nice* has never been part of my vocabulary.

"You better tell me what you want. Not sure the front desk got the memo." Gia's a sweetheart but she's not the most organized person. Probably should get around to firing her but that would require finding a new receptionist. Plus, she's got a great smile and never gives me shit. Wouldn't be easy for her to find another job, either, since she's got a two-year-old and never-ending day care issues.

"A tattoo." She drums the pretty nails that match her toes, foot tapping like she's Queen of Sheba. I'd like to say that imperiousness makes her not my type, but who am I kidding? I fuck anyone who smiles my way. I don't like alone time, commitments or longevity.

"Put my ink right here." She reaches around, pointing to the top of her ass.

I grab my sketchpad from my rolling table. "You got a design in mind? Special occasion to commemorate?"

I ask more to keep her talking. Women like her—ironed, pressed and slumming in East Las Vegas—usually request rainbows or flowers. They demand teeny, tiny piece-of-crap tattoos rather than living large. Sometimes, they ask for the name of a lover or a boyfriend. Dead people and dead relationships are also popular—because if you're not celebrating the hell out of the living, you're mourning their loss.

Not that I have a problem tattooing *Property Of* on
a woman's ass. Fuck no. The problem comes when
she busts back in a week or a month later, demanding I cover the words up with "something pretty."
There's nothing pretty about sex when it's mistaken
for love, and love is as likely as a unicorn and a dodo
bird getting it on.

"The douche," Blondie slurs.

Awesome. Tonight we're celebrating a death and
the douchebag who's blown his chance fatally.

I drop onto my rolling chair, scooting closer. While
Blondie smells as if she's rolled around in a gigantic
strawberry margarita, my face almost brushes my
girl's shoulder before I catch a hint of scent from
her. Something subtle and discreet, the kind of thing
the club girls try on at Macy's because no way can
they afford it for real. Beauty's skin smells like vanilla and coconut, a warm, sweet invitation to eat
her for dessert.

Sitting behind her on my stool, I glimpse her face
in the storefront window. I deliberately brush my
shoulder against hers as I offer her my hand. "Vik.
Pleased to meet you, Harper."

My hands are large, battered and scarred, the
knuckles inked with Cyrillic symbols until there's
not an inch of bare skin. I was born here, but my old
man came over from Russia when he was twenty. He
pulled plenty of shit before and after he patched
into his club, and he made a few introductions on
my behalf after my Navy stint. Those connections
left a mark.

"So you wanna give me more words about what you want?"

"Not flowers and hearts," she says decisively. "Fuck that shit. Today's been a bad day."

"Tell Doctor Vik all about it," I purr.

"I came home from work," she says. "Seems like no big deal, right? Kick off my heels, heat something up, fall into the tub and then bed."

The barest hint of a liquid slur to her words warns me she's not quite sober. I nod, filling in the blanks. Another woman in her bed, a we-need-to-talk moment, a fight. A, B, C, or D—all of the above. Beauty doesn't seem like a screamer, but she also doesn't seem like the kind of woman who gets ink. I grab the Sharpie from my back pocket and uncap it.

"He'd kicked me out."

He being the dead-to-her douchebag.

"Fucker," I say agreeably, tucking her ponytail over her shoulder.

"Absolutely," she agrees. "He had a service pack up my stuff and leave it in the garage for me. I didn't even get to pick and choose which parts of our life I kept. He pointed and strangers put my pieces in boxes. He kept my *cat*."

"I could go over there and kick his ass. Pull a little repo action for you."

A smile ghosts over her mouth. "You have no idea how tempting that is."

"Offer stands." When I smooth my hand over her skin, she jumps. "Touching you is part of my job, babe. Your job is to tell me what you want."

In bed, out of bed, up against the wall—I'm at her command.

"Give me something to celebrate getting free of him even if it wasn't on my terms," she demands.

"How much have you had to drink tonight, sweetheart?"

Her brow puckers as she holds her hands out in front of her. She's wearing a bracelet, a pretty little toy with a heart and key on it. Had that fucker given it to her or had she bought it for herself? "Four. No—five drinks."

"You trust me?"

"Absolutely not," she says, proving she's as smart as she looks. "Tell me what you're thinking."

"Firebird." I drag the Sharpie over her skin, bringing to life the image I see in my head. Maybe she won't appreciate wearing a Russian fairy tale on her skin, but she's not timid; and bold black, orange and red lines tracing the equally strong lines of her back feel right.

"You're a man of few words, Vik." Her lashes drift down as she exhales.

"Don't fall asleep on me."

She shakes her head. "Then don't bore me."

"Bitch," I say tenderly. "Firebird's a thief and hard to catch. She almost gets busted stealing the king's apples when the king sets his sons to catch whoever's been trespassing on his shit. Ivan gets a hand on her, but all he's left with is a single feather. She leaves and he spends fucking forever chasing after her."

"That's the entire story?" She yawns, turning her face into the leather.

"Only part I'm inking here. Yeah?"

"Okay."

I embrace the familiar adrenaline rush as I draw on her lower back, sketching the outline of a bird, wings outstretched to take flight to freedom. Her tail curls down, teasing, flirting, broadcasting a fuck you to the man she's leaving behind in the king's orchard. This is my skin, my piece of her to ink, to own, to give back to her filled up with the story she's shared with me. Right now, I own her and she's mine. She relaxes into my touch, my calloused fingers scraping gently, carefully over her skin, preparing her. Fuck playing by the rules.

I grab my needle and brush my mouth over her ear. "This is gonna hurt so good."

CHAPTER TWO

Harper

VIK DOESN'T REMEMBER ME.

The hottest man I've ever touched—and thank You, Jesus, I've touched this man—introduces himself as if I'm a stranger. As if he's never kissed me, never put his dick inside me, never made me see stars because he felt so damn good. High school seniors, a keg of beer and a wild party were apparently a recipe for oblivion.

Even through the rubber gloves he wears, the heat and strength of him sears me. It's weirdly seductive, his soft touch. Or maybe I'm lonelier than I thought to find comfort in the simple brush of fingers against skin. I'm paying him to give me this contact, and I'm far drunker than I should be if I'm in a tattoo parlor.

Today—tonight—is a day for firsts.

He hums, blond hair falling around his face as he sets the needle against my back. The first touch stings, the bright, rough bite blossoming into something rougher and darker. I push down into the seat to escape the burn but there's no out for me. Why am I here?

Because the man you thought you'd marry locked you out.

Because you do the same things over and over and you want different.

Because your life plan just hit an unexpected brick wall.

The sound that escapes my mouth is embarrassingly weak. I don't have to do this. I can go. He finds new skin with the needle and I whimper.

"Breathe." He pins me in place with one big hand. I should get up. Should tell him I've changed my mind. I had no idea this would hurt so much but when he scratches that needle over my skin, thin, wicked lines cut into me so deep I feel them everywhere. His thumb rubs back and forth over the untouched, un-inked part of me in soft counterpoint.

I twist my head to glare at Brooklyn. "I blame this on you."

She cackles, fishing her phone out of her jacket. Instead of offering sympathy, she immortalizes me for Facebook posterity. "You said you wanted to move on. That you wanted to do something bold and brave to commemorate this particular life milestone."

"I said that after two dirty martinis," I protest.

Vik hums, leaning closer. He hurts me. Part of me wants to kick Brooklyn's ass for talking me into this, but the rest of me just wants Vik closer and closer. To touch me more, to ease the sting his big hands create. Or maybe it's the quiet strength in the way he holds me in place, soothing and hurting and making something beautiful out of the pain.

Thankfully, Brooklyn provides a distraction. "Still counts."

"She's an IRS auditor," I mutter as Brooklyn flips me the bird. She's minutes from passing out hard, her eyes already half-closed.

Behind me, Vik snorts. "That true?"

"Brooklyn doesn't look like a CPA, but trust me. You should be really, really scared if she ever goes through your books. She'll find every secret you tried to hide."

"You could come join me on the dark side," she crows. "But nope. You have to hang with the investment crowd, making all that lovely money. You didn't need the douchebag for his bank account, so I hope the man had a magic dick."

The needles buzz, the pain burning and melting into something fiercer as Vik works. I take a deep breath, counting through the waves of pain. I can do this.

I *want* to do this.

Vik

"Tell me more about this magic dick." Harper tenses as I move the needle over her skin, but a grin lights her face.

"He was pretty," she says. "Everywhere."

Blondie—Brooklyn—raises a brow. "But did he

know what to do with his joystick? Because otherwise it's just a handle to lead him around by."

Harper snickers. "The man could play games for hours. He always made it to the bonus level and he's my all-time highest scorer."

"That's because you hadn't met me yet," I tell her.

Might be a good idea to keep my mouth shut. I consider the possibility for a handful of seconds before discarding it. Why hold back?

"Are you aware that you have no filter?" Harper's hands flex on the bench, opening and closing as she takes what I give her. She starts to say something else, but then winces, sucks in a breath and freezes. This is the point where some people quit, abandoning my chair, and others bitch and curse. You have to ride out the pain, find its rhythm, lose yourself in each wave. There's a magic moment where you pop to the top, finding the crest, and you're fucking flying in a whole other place.

I lay another, deeper line of ink into her skin. "Why putt down the highway of life when you can ride balls-out?"

"Do you like riding, Vik?" Harper's voice is husky and amused, a thread of discomfort just beneath the surface. She has the strangest, sexiest effect on me. I shouldn't want to lean down and kiss each raw line I've etched into her back. Lick the straight, strong line of her spine until she melts for me. She's a client, and whatever fucked-up shit goes on in my head, it stays there.

"Yeah," I say roughly. "I ride. I'm a member of the Hard Riders MC."

"MC?" She turns her head so she can watch my face.

"Motorcycle club."

"Isn't that illegal?"

"Depends on who you're asking, babe. Also on what kind of business we've got. Most days we're practically Boy Scouts. Even do a toy drive at Christmastime."

"And the other days?"

"We take care of business."

I give in to temptation and run my thumb down the straight line of her spine. Woman's got more knots in her back than that macramé shit my brother Cord learned in prison. Supposed to be therapeutic and relaxing as fuck as Cord can attest. He tied up a few strippers and taught them the finer points of bondage when he got out.

"You need to move on." Blondie's words come out soft and slurred. I don't disagree with her, and if Harper wants to forget the douche, I'm the man to help her.

Harper winces as my needle finds a particularly sensitive spot. "How many minutes until we're done?"

"Sweetheart," I say, brushing my mouth over her ear, "we're barely started."

I know firsthand what the needle feels like when it bites through skin, how the pain doesn't ever quite ease up. Shit hurts. Life hurts. But this pain is a choice and it leads to a thing of fucking beauty at the end if I do it right. My firebird slowly takes flight on Harper's back, first the wings, and then the head. I lose myself in between the lines, drawing and coloring, pulling something from her and putting it on the outside for everyone to see.

Harper's quiet for long enough that I lean over to make sure she hasn't passed out on me. Not that she's a constant talker, but some sign of life would be good. Her eyes are closed, her lips parted when I need her to be here with me.

"Hey. You okay?" I drag the back of my knuckles over her cheek, cursing the latex between my skin and hers.

Her lashes lift slowly. She's got the prettiest, softest eyes. "It hurts."

"Good hurt or bad hurt?"

Her forehead gets this cute little pucker like my question doesn't compute. "Good hurt?"

"Yeah. The kind where the burn eats you up and you get lost in all that feeling and you just have to let go and ride it out. You feel me?"

The crease in her forehead deepens, so I'll have to show her. I lay down a new line of ink. She's a squirmer. She wriggles against my bench, working her pussy into the leather like it'll open up and give her a way out of here.

"You chose this," I point out. "You put your cute little ass in my chair. You can endure the pain, or you can let go and lose yourself in it. I think you might like it."

I drag my thumb down the outside of her spine,

working against one of those knots. Investment bank-
ing doesn't sound like a fucking picnic, and her body
seems to agree with me. She lifts into my touch, the
muscle beneath my fingertip loosening. Then she
wiggles against the seat again.

"If this makes you feel better, it's a good thing,"
I say roughly. The ink I'm tracing into her skin certainly is—the bright red feathers almost fly off her
skin, they look so fucking real. "You deserve good
things, you hear me?"

"Yeah," she says, so softly that I almost don't hear
her. "I do."

Blondie's head hits the window with an audible
thunk. I can't tell if she's passed out or fallen asleep,
but girlfriend looks painfully uncomfortable.

"Give me a moment." I set my equipment down
and strip off my gloves. "Sleeping Beauty needs an
assist."

"Sleeping Beauty?" Harper twists her head and
takes in her friend sprawled half on, half off the window seat. Not my circus, not my fucking monkeys,
but she's here with Harper.

I brush my hands down my thighs. "You need a
chaperone?"

Harper outright laughs. "Are you planning on hiding Brooklyn's body?"

"Nah." I shake my head and cross the room to
Blondie. Harper watches like she can't quite figure
me out as I scoop her friend up in my arms. "I'm offering relocation services. Think she'd be more comfortable on the couch."

I take her out front and set her down on the leather couch. Gia never looks up from whatever game she's playing on her phone. The room's chilly from the air-conditioning that ran for most of the day so I shrug out of my leather jacket and drop it over Harper's friend. The nipples poking the front of her sequined tank top advertise loud and proud that the woman's cold. It may be August in Vegas but it's also two in the morning. The sun's not up, and I don't need her to fucking freeze to death—or wake up—before I'm done with Harper.

When I go back into my studio, Harper gives me a smile. The sight of her bent over my bench, waiting for me to put my hands back on her, makes me hard, but then everything about this woman gets me going.

"You're a nice guy." She sounds surprised. Not sure why everyone seems to think bikers do nothing but kill shit. We've got other hobbies and mayhem's just one of my many talents.

"Everybody loves me." I wink at her reflection in Ink Me's windows. "So what does an investment banker do all day, Harper darling?"

"I make other people money."

"Are you good at what you do?" Harper doesn't strike me as the kind of person who'd settle for half-assing anything in life.

"I'm the best." A small, self-satisfied smile licks up the corners of her mouth. I'll bet she goddamned is the best. I know better but I press my fingers a little harder against her skin, spreading them so I can feel the little shivers as the needle bites into her skin and

then the moment when she relaxes. She'd feel like that
when I was deep inside her, too, making her come.

"Me, too." Either you rock your shit, or you don't,
and I'm the best goddamned tattoo artist in Vegas. I
already know that tonight's ink is my best ever. My
firebird looks ready to streak into the sky—or curl
up and dig in because it's hard to imagine a sweeter
spot than the curve of Harper's back.

"This is the hard part," I warn.

Sure enough, when I start shading the feathers, she
tries to hold it all in but a groan escapes her mouth.

"You don't have to pretend for me," I tell her. Mean
it, too. "You do whatever you fucking feel like doing."

She nods—and then she reaches down, feeling for
me with her hand. The fuck? My dick may be hoping
for a hand job, but instead her fingers find my thigh
and pinch. Fucking hard, too. She can't get a good
purchase on me thanks to my jeans and my being built
like a medieval Viking, all hard and no soft.

Christ, she's amazing.

Still, she needs to understand that she doesn't get
to be the one in charge here. "Do that again and I'll
spank your ass."

Not the smartest thing I could say, seeing as how
it doesn't just cross the line of what's appropriate and
what's not. More like my words blow the goddamned
line up and bury it in a mountain of TNT.

"You said I could do whatever I wanted." Did she
just blush? Been a long time since I've been with a
woman who got embarrassed.

"Sure thing." I draw her hand up by her head and

pin it there lightly. "But if you make me jump, sweet-heart, you're gonna end up with a mutant firebird. This next part hurts the worst."

"How long?" I can hear the tears in her voice. Fucking sucks. Harper's made for smiles, not crying.

"Not long. Be good and I'll kiss it better."

"Be specific."

I've got a lot of bare skin to fill in. This won't be quick or easy. "Forty minutes."

"Are you shitting me?" She shifts and I back off.

"Kisses," I remind her. "I'll make everything feel better if you hang in here."

"You've got magic kisses?" That's her drunk talk-ing, laughter blurring the edges of her words and pushing away the tears.

"You can find out."

"I already know how you kiss," she announces, that cute pink blush getting deeper. "We've met be-fore."

Shit. I rack my brain trying to remember her. Women come and go in my life. Pretty sure I wouldn't have fucked Harper and forgotten her, though, so maybe she's just messing with me. Fair enough, see-ing as how I'm planning on getting her out of those cute little panties just as soon as I can.

"That so? We've shared adult naptime? Done the bedroom rodeo?" I start in on the skin over her spine.

"It doesn't matter." She shrugs like whatever mem-ories she's got are NBFD—no big fucking deal—and I tap her ass.

"Freeze," I remind her. "Or you'll make me color

outside the lines. And while you're holding that thought, give me details about what we did together."

"Nope." Now I get the smile I wanted earlier, a big, wicked grin that lights up her entire face.

"A hint," I suggest.

"We met in high school," she concedes.

Huh. I do some more thinking while I work on her ink. High school wasn't my finest moment. I was too busy being angry at the world to stop and think. Used my fists, my mouth, my dick—whatever got the biggest rise out of my audience. Guess Harper here must have been on the receiving end of my dick.

"Tell me all about it."

"Not a chance." I see her roll her eyes in the window. I forgo smacking her ass, seeing as how we're in a public venue and all. I don't need the shit Prez would give me if the club's lawyers had to get me out of an assault charge. Instead, I try my words again. I can work miracles with my tongue, but that's in the eating-her-out department. Once I start working her clit over, she'll tell me what I want to know.

Not that *she* seems to remember things that way.

"You don't want to piss off the guy holding the needle, sweetheart."

She narrows her eyes. "I'm paying you. You have to do what I say."

Christ, she makes me laugh. "Do I look like I follow the rules? Remind me."

She rolls her eyes. "You're impossible."

"But you like me."

"And you don't remember me," she counters. "At all."

"I was your best, right? So fucking awesome that the Douche couldn't hope to compare?" I squeeze her shoulder with my free hand. I can feel her bra strap beneath the silky fabric, so I nudge it downward an inch just to piss her off. "No. Don't tell me. I'll guess."

CHAPTER THREE

Harper

"MOVE YOUR HAND and I won't have to sue you."

The words fly out of my mouth automatically, the way you blurt out *excuse me* when you stand on a stranger's foot in the train or accidentally slam your boob into someone. They're just words, things that should be said. I have no clue what I'd do if he actually acted on them.

Okay.

I might know.

I suspect—but can't confirm—I'd beg him to keep on touching me because he's right about one thing. The pain has melted into something else, a throbbing, hot sensation that makes me squirm against the leather seat and imagine dirty, depraved acts. It's wrong. It's completely unprofessional and I'm entirely certain I could be thrown out of Ink Me with a half-finished tattoo on my back for propositioning the talent and getting the seat all wet.

"You're really not gonna tell me?" Swear to God,

the man is pouting—and he's got the face for it. He could model for an underwear company. His billboard would stop traffic, he's so damned pretty. I had no idea I was this shallow but his cheekbones and that mouth… I'd happily look at every inch of him, in or out of his briefs.

I really need to have sex again.

"We did it in the gym," he suggests, big hands moving over my skin. I know he's just doing his job, but I'm having the most inappropriate feelings for him. Fortunately he has no filter himself.

"Earth to Harper." He taps my back to get my attention. "Did you check out like this when we made love? Because you might have scarred me."

Ordinarily, his inability to recall me—naked no less—would be humiliating, but my recent breakup with Mark has set the bar high.

"Definitely the gym," Vik murmurs. He's changed since that night in high school—filled out and gotten even bigger. The football coach was always after him to play, although he never would.

"You think?" The constant pleasure-burn of the needle loosens something inside me and not just my tongue. I can't hold on to any kind of anger right now. It leaches out of me.

"Yeah." I see Vik nod in the window. His hair slides around his face, longer and sun-bleached, a thick, shaggy mane better suited to a tiger or some kind of wild animal. "Bet we got nasty on the mats beneath the bleachers. Bet you were worried someone might walk in on us."

"Not the gym." The needle bites into my skin again, but the burn isn't so bad now. It's a deep, insistent rhythm of its own, this sharp scratching as he remakes me.

He's silent for a moment, but he's not done. "Empty classroom, then. Fucking loved those big teacher desks they had."

"You didn't." God, I hope no one did the whole apple-for-the-teacher thing after he'd done the nasty. Talk about unsanitary.

"I can't believe I don't remember you." I have to give him credit. He sounds like he means it.

I point out the obvious, however. "Maybe you have a volume problem."

He winks at me in the glass. "Practice makes perfect."

I roll my eyes. "There's a time and a place for overachieving. Do you even know how many girls you've slept with?"

"Do you know?" he counters.

"Zero," I say promptly. "Absolutely no girls."

"Tell me it's not so." He sighs. "All guys know that you college girls go wild and crazy in your dorms as soon as it's lights-out. Tell me you lived at home and I'll forgive you."

"On campus. All four years. Pick a new fantasy."

"Do you promise to help me reenact it?"

"When hell freezes over," I say companionably. This is crazy. Despite our brief but memorable (on my part, anyhow) past, I don't really know Vik. He's changed, I've changed and his idea of conversation would get me fired at my own job. On the other hand, I wanted to start over. New Me is getting her very first tattoo because Old Me wouldn't have so much as glanced at a tattoo parlor. So perhaps New Me can also trade witty sex jokes with the crazy-hot tattoo artist. New Me wouldn't give it up in the back seat of a Dodge Charger and then head home panty-less. If nothing else, New Me will be a thong girl all the way.

I think about this to pass the time, but there's only so long I can meditate on my past underwear choices. The more Vik works, the harder it gets to stay still. No one warned me that getting a tattoo sounds way too much like we're having sex. The sound of his hands brushing over my skin is followed by the rush of my breath as I exhale a little harder. Bite back a moan when he finds a particularly sensitive spot with his needle. I'm not quite to the point of screaming *oh, oh, oh*…but I'm getting there.

"Can I ask a question?" he says eventually.

Thank God. At this point I'd take a recitation of the dictionary from front to back over the interesting sensations building up where he's touching me. Especially since those sensations don't seem to stay put—they insist on migrating lower.

Because he's inking my lower back, his hands brush the top of my butt. It's unavoidable. It doesn't mean anything, but certain parts of me take notice. Plus, there's the delicious, wicked burn of the needle. At first the needle hurts, but as I relax into the sting, the feeling changes.

Because even if it hurts, it also feels good.

I want him to do it again and again, so that I can figure out why I like this. He lays another line of ink against my skin, and this time I push up toward him rather than away. The burn becomes something else, a heated sensation that's mine, that I own, that I crave.

I've never been into kink. I'm as vanilla and boring as they come and I don't *mind* that. I like who I am. I may be vanilla cake with cream cheese frosting surrounded by more exotic, colorful flavors, but I go with everything. As long as you're in the mood for cake, I never disappoint.

And yet my panties are wet and the sensations get stronger and better until I'm fighting not to clench or rub myself against the bench.

"Your boyfriend broke up with you, right?"

"Yeah." I'd really rather not think about that right now.

"So how come you're the one who's out on the street, looking for a new place to live?"

You know what? I don't have a good answer for that. I take a stab at it anyhow.

"Because his name was on our lease?"

Vik makes a dismissive noise. "If he's the one who wants change, he changes. You stay and he goes."

It's dark outside, and the few people walking past the window are either staggeringly drunk or so wrapped up in each other that they don't look inside Ink Me's windows. It's liberating knowing that everyone and no one is watching, that Vik and I are alone in this pool of light inside a bigger sea of darkness. I suddenly understand why all those detectives in

TV shows shine a spotlight on their targets, willing them to speak.

The words spill out of me with each question that Vik asks. He can't care about my answers, not really. He's working, filling the minutes and the silence the same way he colors in the blank spots on my skin, and yet it feels both surreal and good at the same time. It has nothing to do with my noticing how powerful his thighs are in those wash-worn, threadbare jeans of his, or how his motorcycle boots make me think really, really dirty thoughts.

"There was no magic putty for my relationship with Mark. The problem is I get distracted by a pretty face and Mark had that in spades."

"I'll be your booty call," he says as he presses a bandage over my lower back.

"Excuse me?"

I sound like I have a stick up my butt. Prissy. Uptight.

And he repeats the utterly ridiculous, totally crazy thing he just said.

"If you need a pretty face for sex, you can call me."

CHAPTER FOUR

Harper

VIK SHOVES A tattooed hand in my face. "Up," he says.

His voice is phenomenal. Low and rough, full of heat and humor, the man could make a fortune as a sex line worker. He could read bedtime stories, dirty limericks, the stock report...anything, and I'd be jilling off on the other end of the line because he's that goddamned sexy.

Danger, danger.

Getting up is exponentially harder than lying down. Not only am I more sober, but I'm stiff. There's also the whole business of my skirt and my blouse, and even though what goes up must come down, my skirt is a challenge. The fabric clings to my legs, and the strong possibility of flashing my high school lover-turned-biker my cotton-covered butt makes me self-conscious. Frankly, I'd feel better about putting myself on display if I wasn't wearing sensible white cotton.

Vik solves my logistical issues for me. Large hands

close around my waist and yank me upward. I try not to giggle, but a squeak escapes me anyhow. I'm painfully ticklish, and his fingers dig gently into every spot I wish he'd avoid. At least he's quick. I don't even have time to worry about the doughnuts I've been stress-eating because he flies me through the air and sets me gently on my feet. I'm not a small woman; I started growing up when I was ten and then out two years later. And while I haven't achieved Jolly Green Giant proportions, I'm not precisely sylph-like, either. I'm tall, I'm sturdy *and* I'm wearing four-inch heels.

"Warning would be good." I dig my nails into his forearms trying to find my balance. The skin beneath the dark scrolls of ink is sun-bronzed. It's also totally lickable, but I need to *not* think about that.

"Vik Air at your service," he deadpans. "Although you either have to let go or come home with me."

We both look down at the death grasp I have on his arms.

Right.

I let go.

Vik strips off his gloves and tosses them into the trash. I guess we're done here. He might be hot and talented, but this isn't personal. Sure, I've felt this man's hands on my body, his breath on my skin for three hours, but it's a business deal. His ink in exchange for my money. Anything else was absolutely not on the price list the girl at the front desk gave me.

But I want more.

God help me, but I do. I don't want tonight to end. Right now, it feels like I've lost everything. In the morning, I'll end my pity party, but right now, I don't remember what's right with my life. I just remember the crap. I don't have my place anymore. My stuff's packed up in a storage pod. My ex hijacked our Siamese. All I have is work on Monday and…this night. The tattoo, this man's hands on me waking me up in places I didn't know I was asleep. Would you want it to end? If I'd been Cinderella, I'd have stuck around on the top of those stairs.

He steers me away from his bench, his hand low and firm just beneath the spot that burns and aches from his needles. And okay, just above another, slightly more southern spot that also aches and burns because clearly I'm all kinds of messed up.

"Harper?" His mouth brushes the hair by my ear.

"Yeah?" My stupid feet stop moving toward the front desk, where an astronomical bill waits for tonight's piece of folly. Ink and this man do not come cheap.

"I'm sorry I don't remember you and I mean it. I'd be happy to be your booty call," he whispers roughly. "All you have to do is ask, sweetheart."

I just…can't.

Vik disappears while I settle up with his receptionist for my new ink. I shouldn't be disappointed. Obviously, the flirty come-on lines are just part of the service—kind of like a hairdresser chatting you up while you're in her chair and pretending she's superinterested in your life. I force myself not to look around while Gia runs my credit card. After I sign the receipt, however, I discover a logistical problem.

Brooklyn's sound asleep on the couch.

Since leaving her here would be a gross violation of the girlcode (we're besties even if she didn't talk me out of getting a tattoo), I need to get her home. And while I definitely outweigh her, I can't deadlift her. While I consider and abandon constructing a travois out of her borrowed jacket and hauling her ass home, Gia disappears with a little wave. Guess it's quitting time at the zoo.

I could drag Brooklyn outside. The odds of that causing physical damage, however, seem high.

While I'm weighing bruises against camping in a tattoo shop overnight, a bike roars up, the noise of the pipes bouncing off buildings. Vik seems even larger and wilder straddling the enormous bike, which I figure out fast because my eyes just keep checking out his thighs, those long, muscled legs that end in the sexiest pair of boots, the powerful forearms that effortlessly guide the bike to a stop. I can't stop looking, which in retrospect probably should be a red flag that this man isn't easy. That he's capable of riding all over my nice, tidy, way-too-single life as easily as he does the road.

I should have run out of Ink Me screaming.

Instead, I watch him swing off the bike and stride toward me. Possibly, I entertain a few fantasies about pillaging Vikings and village maidens. The fun parts, not the shitty moments involving murder and mayhem. Of course, Mr. Beautiful has no clue about the daydreams playing out inside my head. He's just being a Boy Scout and making sure I'm sorted before he leaves for the night and whatever fun, sexy stuff bad-boy bikers who look like Vikings do in their downtime.

"Called you a taxi," he says when he gets to me, reaching out to touch my arm lightly. The man is definitely snugglier than a cat. A really, really friendly alley cat, I remind myself. Even in high school, his dick had its own frequent flyer club.

"Thanks," I blurt out while he stares patiently at me.

"You want me to follow you home and carry Sleeping Beauty inside?"

"Do you follow all your clients home?"

"Only the cute ones." He winks.

I think about that for a moment too long. Nope. I've got nothing. Flirty banter is not something I excel at—I have a goddamned finance degree from Cornell. Sexy Quips 101 was *not* part of my Ivy League curriculum. Instead, I reexamine Brooklyn, hoping she's magically decided to wake up, sober up and get up.

No such luck.

She snort-sighs, settling deeper into the leather couch. Vik laughs.

"She's out for the night."

Thank you, Captain Obvious.

He puts all those gorgeous muscles to good use, however, sliding his arms underneath her and scooping her up against his chest. They look perfect together, a beautiful blond god and goddess pairing. Her hair trails over his arm as he heads for the door. This is my cue to follow him, and since exhaustion is hitting me hard now, I do. If he's got a solution for my Brooklyn problem, I'll take it.

When we get outside, the taxi is just pulling up. Vik juggles his load of sleeping blonde, and says something to the driver. The guy nods, money changes hands, and then Vik walks around the car, pops open the back door and slides Brooklyn inside. When I open my mouth to protest about his paying, he cuts me off.

"Duane here is gonna see you back to your place. He can carry Sleeping Beauty in if she needs it."

I shouldn't find his ruthless, roughshod side attractive. I blame the broad shoulders stretching the leather of his jacket, or maybe it's the way he leans in to buckle up Brooklyn. He's big but he makes me feel both safe *and* sexy. He's just playing around, but it's been a long time since any guy made me feel like the queen of sexy. Like I don't have to try harder or do more because I'm enough right now, just as I am. I thought I'd have to wait until I met my Mr. Right to feel like that. Looking back, I guess that should've been my first clue that Mark wasn't the guy for me.

"Give me your address." Vik flashes me a wicked smile and I'm grateful I don't have to admit how wet my panties are.

I shoot him a look. He grins. Waiting. I heat up some more. "Because the driver needs it?"

Damn, the man has a sexy laugh. It's low and rough, a dirty, happy-sounding chuckle. I smile back as he saunters back around the car.

"Because I want it, sweetheart."

My girl parts decide this is the best reason ever. In fact, we should totally give Vik whatever he wants. Immediately.

Stupid.

"I'm at the Bellagio," I admit. "I'm between places at the moment thanks to the Douche."

Vik opens the door on my side and hands me in. I'm no dating virgin, but this is the first time any guy has ever physically steered me into a car. I look up at him, intending to protest, and lose my breath. God, he's gorgeous. Gorgeous and so, so close. I can see firsthand that his eyes are still a dark, hard gray…and those beautiful eyes make me forget all about his appropriation of my elbow—and my free will.

My butt hits the seat oh-so-obediently, but he doesn't let go. He cups my elbow with his palm, his fingers stroking briefly over my forearm. It's hardly pornographic but it's been a long time since anyone touched me. Or wanted to. I know Mark didn't, because our California King–size bed had stricter borders than North and South Korea. Mark hadn't crossed those lines to my side of the bed in months.

Vik retreats, shuts the door and then leans down, his big, tattooed hands curling around the open window frame. "Got a proposition for you."

"Okay." I'd like to pretend I don't sound breathless, but this man is like fine wine. He's only gotten better since high school.

"We're having a party out at the clubhouse tomorrow night. Think you'd have fun if you came out."

Is he asking me out on a date? Or maybe this is

the biker version of a coffee? In theory we're old high school friends who haven't seen each other in years, so this could be strictly platonic, or him just being nice because he's aware my life is a mess.

"You're thinking too hard." He looks amused as he pulls a business card out of his jacket pocket and scribbles an address on it. He takes my hand, tucking the card into my palm and closing my fingers around it. His thumb strokes over my knuckles briefly. "Say *yes*. I promise I won't forget you this time."

His eyes dip to my mouth. Is he thinking about kissing me? Am *I* thinking about kissing *him*?

"Maybe," I blurt out, my good intentions melting like my panties.

I'm still trying to decide as he saunters back to his bike, straddles the seat and rides off. Usually, I'd just admire the view and get on with my life, but nothing about today has been normal. I've been rendered homeless, dumped and inked. And after an evening of downing way too many cocktails, I've also got a monster-size thirst to go with the start of a headache—and the contacts I've been wearing all day aren't helping. Hooking up with a biker and tattoo artist is also something I wouldn't usually do.

But I'm painfully aware that the man's ass and thighs are a delicious work of art that deserve appreciating. Biker. Charmer. Player. Vik is all of these and more, and the sex appeal just rolls off him. Maybe we could hook up, but it couldn't end any better than it did the first time.

Trouble.

That's what Vik is. He's Capital T Trouble.

He's not the Mr. Right I've been searching for, he doesn't fit into my life plan, and that makes him most definitely not the person I need in my life right now. If I were smart, I'd sit out on dating for a few months even if said life plan calls for marriage and kids before I'm thirty-five and my eggs start drying up like water in the desert. It's just that I'd swear Vik looked at me like he liked what he saw. I mean, really, *really* liked what he saw. And he walked me out and gave me his card and God I need to find a life somewhere. I've already taken his dick for a ride, so it's not like I can even blame curiosity for the warm sensation licking my belly and melting all my resolve.

I settle slowly into the seat as the taxi pulls away from Ink Me. Brooklyn makes a face like she's giving serious consideration to puking, so I rub her back and try to not hear the wounded animal sounds she's making.

I should throw Vik's card away. Instead, I turn it over. It's the general card for Ink Me, with all the basic contact information for hitting up the tattoo parlor for an appointment. On the reverse side, however, Vik has scrawled an address and two words.

Come over.

Oh, and he's also sketched a cartoon Viking that's...

Doing something downright obscene.

To a very large penis.

That has...

Ink?

I shove the card into my purse and try not to wonder if Vik has tattoos in some very personal areas. How likely is it that a guy would let a needle and ink anywhere near his favorite body part? Plus, the pain. And how would that even work? Do you ink when you're hard or soft?

He has to be exaggerating.

I make a mental note to Google penis sizes and hand-to-dick ratios. After that, I'll clear my browser cache and get on with my life, curiosity satisfied.

Really.

I will.

Bad boys and bankers don't mix.

CHAPTER FIVE

Harper

MY LIFE DOES not magically sort itself out overnight.

This comes as no surprise, although part of me wishes I'd inherit a fairy godmother or some magic beans. Instead, I wake up alone in my Bellagio hotel room. Since I'm only here for a week or two until I find a new place and I'm paying for my reservation with the Douche's lifetime hoard of frequent flyer miles, I upgraded to a room with a fountain view. This means I don't even have to get out of bed to see the watery fireworks. One push of a convenient bedside button and the blackout drapes part with a dramatic swoosh, sunlight pouring inside as the water below shoots upward to the sounds of "Lucy in the Sky with Diamonds."

I go all in and order room service pancakes. A pot of overpriced coffee, hothouse strawberries and a pound of butter improve my mood substantially. I send emails and make calls, setting up appointments to view various condos because unfortunately I can't live at the Bellagio forever.

I do Saturday things after I've done what I can to organize my life, because it would be a shame to be camped out at the Strip's fanciest hotel and not take advantage of it. I swim in pools surrounded by faux-Grecian statuary spouting water. I lose ten bucks in the slot machines. I pass on visiting the art gallery in favor of the ginormous chocolate fountain in the hotel's candy shop because everything is better with chocolate.

And the whole time I keep thinking about last night. About Vik's casual invitation to join him at an MC party. He might be hot and uninhibited, but he's also a biker, and he's the guy who banged me in the back seat of his car after high school prom...and then promptly forgot my name, my face and every detail of that encounter. I've probably idealized his bedroom skills. He's not worth pursuing, and he likely has zero interest in me that way, even if he did offer to be my booty call. Who says those kinds of things?

Other than company events, I can't remember the last party I went to. There aren't many festive moments on my calendar. Okay, so I could swing by Vik's clubhouse and check out his party. My night's wide-open, and how many opportunities will I get to ogle an entire roomful of bikers? Since I'm most definitely not drinking tonight, I could even drive there, which would give me a handy escape route. I'm assuming a biker event is a little rowdier and grittier than, say, a fund-raiser ball, and it's entirely possible I'll feel too uncomfortable to do more than just look in.

I go through the clothes I've stashed in the closet. Most of them are work things, with a healthy side of yoga pants. Nothing screams *party*. I do a quick Google search for biker get-together dress codes but come up mostly empty. Lots of leather and denim, plus the occasional porn- or Coachella-worthy outfit that makes Princess Leia's slave girl bikini look like a nun's habit.

Huh.

Going naked—or even mostly naked—seems like it would send the wrong message, plus I can't picture myself strutting around in denim shorts and a black bikini top. Maybe it's all in the footwear?

I could go shopping.

Something tells me that Vik would really enjoy a pair of fuck-me Louboutins, for instance. Or I could wear yesterday's heels.

But I feel like something new to go with the new me.

I end up calling Brooklyn for a consult, and then she meets me in the lobby and we hit the Desert Passage Shops at the Aladdin. There's an awesome bar smack in the middle of the mall like the best kind of desert oasis. We make a well-deserved pit stop there for yard-long frozen margaritas that come in fluorescent yellow bongs and manage to achieve both quantity and quality.

After that, we hit the shops. Brooklyn insists that I need to go for a whole new look, and I'm in the mood for a change. She grabs an armload of insanely teeny clothes off the rack in a store I've never stepped foot in before. It's the kind of place that advertises on the pages of *Vogue*, and I'm pretty sure the fabulously gorgeous clothes will be wasted on a bunch of bikers. So it's a good thing I'm dressing for me now.

I come home with a ridiculously expensive black tube top and a pair of wicked stiletto booties with ribbons instead of laces. Outside of work, I avoid anything that adds to my height, but new me, new rules, and apparently New Me has decided tonight's theme is girlish bondage. I shimmy into a pair of skinny jeans that seem to have gotten smaller since their last wash, and then I hit the road.

Vik's clubhouse is not exactly on the Strip. In fact, it's most definitely in East Las Vegas, and the blocks get grittier and more dangerous as I get closer. It's the kind of neighborhood with bars on the windows, bright splashes of graffiti and cars up on blocks. Pots of succulents and geraniums line the walkways adding some hopeful color, and more than one strand of white twinkling lights wrap around palm trees despite the summer weather. Eventually, the houses give way to block after block of slightly run-down, gone-to-seed warehouses. In the movies, this is the point where the bad guys come out shooting or there are gratuitous explosions.

The GPS on my phone announces it's time to turn. I'm not sure what I expected, but Vik's clubhouse looks like all the other warehouses—except for the parking lot full of bikes. Who needs a sign reading Biker Party Here or a clutch of helium balloons with all those Harleys reeking of testosterone?

The bikers themselves don't seem too scary. I mean, they're definitely not firemen, or lawyers, or anything remotely wholesome-looking or suit-wearing, but they're also not engaged in any visible felonies, which I appreciate. They're simply a bunch of guys milling around the bikes, talking and joking. The dress code appears to call for leather and boots. Music pounds out of the warehouse when someone pulls the door open. I don't recognize the singer, but the song has one of those hard-hitting, pulse-raising beats that makes you want to dance in place or screw.

I so don't belong here.

Nevertheless, one of the younger bikers waves me into an empty spot next to a row of trucks. I spot a Camaro, a Dodge Charger and a dented-up minivan that looks about as bikerly as I do, so there's hope for my evening after all. Perhaps the Hard Riders practice a more inclusive form of clubbing?

When I get out, the fresh-faced biker gives me a nod. "You looking for someone?"

I'll bet they don't get too many party-crashers. "Vik."

"Inside," he says. I think he smirks—or possibly rolls his eyes. I'm clearly not the first woman to ask after Vik tonight. "Probably in back by the bar. Might be spinning."

I lock my car (although I'm not sure that's going to stop anyone) and head for the clubhouse. The front door is much more imposing and formidable than the parking lot attendant. In fact, it's clearly been built for mega-giants, and I wrestle with it for a long moment, my glasses sliding down my nose.

A thick, inked arm reaches over me and shoves it open.

"Ladies first," the arm's owner drawls. He looks me up and down slowly, taking in my jeans and dressy boots. I suddenly know how a zebra feels when it accidentally steps into a lion's den. The look on this guy's face is part amusement, part hunger. I'd like to tell him I'm not a steak, but the patch on his vest says PRESIDENT, and I have a feeling that makes him the king of this particular kingdom. If he says I'm steak, I'm steak.

"Is this your club?" I like to know who's in charge, but Mr. I'm-Gonna-Eat-You-Up seems to find my question funny because he just snorts and reaches down to shove my glasses back into place.

"Yeah. I'm Prez. You got an issue with that, sunshine?"

I think about that for a minute and shake my head. Despite my invitation, coming out here seems less smart all the time. Some women like living dangerously, but I've never been one of them. I prefer my life safe and sane, which begs the question of what I'm doing here. Starting over. Taking a chance. About to suffer public humiliation. You can take your pick, but my car and escape looks better and better.

"In," he rumbles, his hand pressing against my shoulder. I decide not to protest, and move forward.

Prez follows me inside, so close that the front of his thighs brush the back of mine. I don't think that's an accident. He cups my elbow, herding me in the direction he wants me to go. This whole life-changing stuff is stupid. Take-charge guys have never been my thing. *Except Vik*, a little voice whispers in my head. *You like* him.

I'm working on that.

You hear things about motorcycle clubs and the Hard Riders have a certain reputation, or so my Google-fu tells me. While they look after their own and spend a commendable amount of time giving back to their community (Vik wasn't kidding about the Christmas toy drive), they also ride hard and party harder. There are darker rumors and whispers, too, about how they have a zero-tolerance policy on drugs and are key players in East Las Vegas's war on illegal substances—although it appears they're big fans of beer.

The place is definitely not the bat cave.

Music blasts from the back of the warehouse. The clubhouse is huge, the entire downstairs floor open and jammed with gyrating, dancing, drinking bodies. Lots of black leather couches have been pushed back against the wall to open up a path to the makeshift bar in the back. Longnecks and red Solo cups are the order of the day. As is skin. I've never seen this much skin on display outside of a beach or a Vegas strip revue. As I scan the crowd, looking for Vik, I realize I'm overdressed.

In fact, clothing seems to be largely optional and I could have saved the money I spent on my shopping trip and just worn my underwear. A brunette in what could be a tube top or a dress brushes past us. The stretchy fabric barely skims her butt, and that's *before* she squeals and throws herself at her dance partner. She scissors her legs around his waist. Everyone here is loud and uninhibited.

A red cup dangles in front of my face.

I take it. I don't know where it came from, so I'm not drinking it but I need something to do with my hands, and I'm *definitely* not doing what the brunette is doing. "Thanks?"

Prez winks at me. "Who're we lookin' for?"

He's got a soft, smoky burr of an accent that makes me think of warm Louisiana nights and the bayou. It's the kind of drawl that almost but not quite distracts you from the fact that this is the guy who runs a biker club and could probably have you killed with one nod of his head.

I really should care about that. Instead, I pony up the answer he's looking for. "Vik."

Prez rubs his free hand over his chin, his pained sigh gusting over my skin. "Figures."

I want to ask what that means, but I'm distracted by the madman bouncing around the dance floor. Shoulder-length blond hair flies everywhere. Vik dances all-out. Muscular, inked arms cut through the air as he thrashes to a beat that bears no resemblance whatsoever to the music vibrating through the warehouse. Faded blue jeans hug his ass and end in a pair of motorcycle boots. Just in case the gift-wrapping on that particular part of the package doesn't scream *open me*, he's wearing his club vest over a fitted white

T-shirt. Muscles bulge as he executes another move and part of me wants to hang all over that arm. See how good it feels. Shove it between my legs.

I'm not the only one with that idea.

A skinny, fabulously gorgeous woman in a barely there black leather dress shimmies up to him and starts using him as her own personal dance pole. They're so close that her breasts press up against his arm and she's riding his thigh as she grinds high and bumps low. I'm so glad I made the effort to come tonight.

And apparently Vik prefers quantity to quality because not one but two more wanna-be dancers latch onto him as he burns up the dance floor. I feel like I should be pulling a wad of one-dollar bills out of my purse and rewarding their efforts.

"Is he always like this?" The words fly out of my mouth before I can stop them.

Prez chuckles. "Pretty much. Man's the fucking Energizer Bunny when it comes to gettin' laid."

Just great.

I take a step backward and bump awkwardly into Prez. Shit. Naturally, my reaction is to lurch forward to put some space between my butt and his groin. Prez laughs again, his hands steadying my hips as I rock on my stupid high heels. He bellows Vik's name, the sound all but getting lost in the general chaos and uproar that is a biker party. Not that I was expecting to be announced by trumpets or a twenty-one-gun salute, but still.

Miracle of miracles, Vik looks toward us. A

wicked grin lights up his face and he dumps the leg-humper off his thigh.

"Harper!" he yells back. His inside voice is loud enough to carry over the deafening beat of the music. So loud that heads turn to stare at me. I consider beating a hasty retreat, but New Me insists on sticking around. She's either brave or horny, and I'm not sure I want to find out which.

Prez chuckles and pats me on the *butt*. "See you later, sunshine."

In a weird way, I don't mind it because the gesture seems less like a creepy grope and more like a friendly overture. Maybe these guys just don't have normal social skills. Or were never housebroken.

Vik bounds over, throwing his arms out. "You found me."

"I did."

People—*bikers*—are still staring.

Possibly, it's because I'm wearing more clothing than all of Vik's previous companions combined. I look down quickly just to make sure that I am fully dressed and not having one of those living nightmares where you waltz into a room buck naked.

I throw caution to the wind and take a sip of my drink, hoping it's magic. A potion like *Alice in Wonderland*'s Drink Me, except maybe it will make me articulate. Give me the gift of gab so that I know what to say to this man. This gorgeous, hot biker who ties me up in knots. Of course, I consumed way more alcohol last night and look how that ended up. I have a tattoo on my back.

Vik grabs my hand. "Dance with me, Harper."

I wait for my drink to kick in, but no luck. Red punch and a truly impressive amount of grain alcohol will not be riding to my rescue tonight.

"Do I look like I dance?" The pole-dancing, thigh-humping antics of his previous partners are not part of my repertoire.

The corners of his mouth quirk up.

I sort of hate him for the way my panties promptly get wet.

Vik sets his hands on my hips—my *hips*—and tugs me closer. He links his hands on top of my butt, fingers skating dangerously close to inked territory, and then he rests his forehead against mine.

"You don't have to dance well," he whispers. I'm pretty sure his mouth brushes my hair. My cup is jammed between us and I have no idea what to do with my spare hand.

"Okay?" New Me, I remind myself. She might turn out to be an awesome closet dancer, so I should make the effort to find out. My feet are still rooted to the floor, though, when somebody jostles us and I slop punch on the front of Vik's shirt. His *white* shirt. Kill. Me.

"God, I, shoot…" I scrub at the front of his shirt. The stain is approximately the size and shape of North America. Possibly South America, too. This is why I don't get asked to parties.

"Hey." He nudges my chin up with his thumb. "No big deal."

He's so beautiful.

I blame my embarrassing muteness on his face. He's the most gorgeous man I've ever seen and he's within touching distance. When he removes his thumb from my face, I almost sigh in disappointment.

And then he flashes a devilish wink at me and shrugs out of his vest. "Hold this for me, babe."

The leather vest he drops into my hands is warm from his skin. You know how there are moments when you can feel your whole life pivot? Because the universe has just served you a red letter day and you need to stop and memorialize that date in your journal? Maybe slap some washi tape and gold stars on that bad boy so that when you look back, fifty years from now, you'll know to tell your grandkids about the day you met dear old granddad and how the trumpets blared and the angelic hosts all pointed at him and declared him to be The One?

I wish I could tell you that's what happens here. I wish I could say I looked at Vik and knew he was a good man and that together we'd have something meaningful.

But I can't.

I am, however, 100 percent in lust with him.

Just look at him.

How could any woman resist?

He hauls his T-shirt over his head in one smooth move and the man could do underwear ads. He's got the most amazing six-pack, all cut muscles dusted with the finest of golden hairs. And the fact that I know this only proves that I'm standing way too close to him. I imagine this must be how Eve looked at

Adam the day she realized he had a dick and he was naked. My gaze travels down in pure appreciation. And then goes down some more until all those *pure* feelings of admiration melt into something far dirtier and hotter. Dear God, the man has been blessed.

"If you wanted me naked, all you had to do was ask."

And just like that he short-circuits the remaining brain cells in my stupid, besotted head. Smacking myself upside my head sounds like a plan, except I need whatever thinking power remains up there. Logic is my new best friend. Calm. I probably should have taken one of those yoga classes where they teach you how to be all Zen and in the moment because right now I'm practically hyperventilating.

Vik isn't helping. He tugs his vest out of my hands (I don't particularly want to give it back), shrugs it on and then tosses the dirty T-shirt onto the floor. "Come on."

I shove my tongue back into my mouth and let him lead where he will. Which is apparently from one group of bikers to the next. And surprisingly, everyone I meet is pretty chill. They tip their heads at me or wink or flash a killer grin, and…I'm having a good time. Plus, Vik turns out to be more of a cuddler than a humper or a groper (contrary to his dance floor exhibition). He keeps an arm around me, squeezing me up against his side as he steers us from group to group. Since he's mostly naked from the waist up, I find this contact deeply distracting.

The last guy we approach is a biker leaning against

the wall. He's every bit as tattooed, hard and lethal-looking as my Vik. His dark hair is buzzed close to his scalp, and the way he watches us has me convinced he could describe us with perfect accuracy to a police sketch artist. Despite his casual slouch, I get the sense that he's entirely aware of his surroundings and more than prepared to take out or take down anything and anyone that becomes a problem.

Tread carefully.

"Rev." Strong fingers close carefully around mine. His grip is firm but pleasant, and I sense he's being careful not to overwhelm me or squeeze too hard. Or maybe it's just the air of cool containment. This is definitely not a man to fuck with.

Vik's eyes narrow. "I'm going to count to three. If you want to keep all those fingers, you let go before I finish, you feel me?"

Rev laughs. "Feeling possessive?"

Vik nods vigorously. "I'm her booty call. She doesn't have time for you."

"I. We—"

I can feel my face going up in flames, but Rev just laughs.

"She had me undressed within minutes of arriving." Vik gestures down his chest with his hand. As if anyone could have missed all those glorious, naked muscles. And the ridges…the tempting, tempting ridges of his perfect abdomen.

I finally manage to wipe the drool off my chin and respond. "You are *not* my booty call."

Vik winks. "I offered. You didn't say no. Plus, I'm totally fine with you using me for sex."

I think he means it.

This just makes my face redder, which makes Rev laugh harder. It's a vicious cycle, and another example of why I have no business being at a biker party. Vik snags my hand and starts towing me deeper into the clubhouse. Eventually, we hit the bar at the back of the building. It's louder here, the music a deep, throbbing bass that I can feel pulsing through the floor beneath my feet. It's a wonder everyone here isn't permanently deaf.

Vik snags a barstool, deposits me on it before I can protest and then leans back against the bar. His shoulder bumps mine as he grabs my hand and starts playing with my fingers.

"You get a place sorted out yet?"

"I've only been homeless for two days," I point out. I excel at multitasking and getting stuff done, but even I have my limits. "I've got appointments tomorrow to look at a few rentals."

"You could move in with me."

I choke on my drink and he pounds me on the back, careful to avoid my new ink.

"Too fast?" He takes the cup and sets it down on the bar.

"Yes," I wheeze. "When did we discuss this?"

"What?" He blinks at me innocently, but his eyes twinkle.

"Sex. Booty calls. *Moving in*."

"Yesterday." He settles his hands on my thighs and

pushes gently. My stupid knees part like the Red Sea and he takes full advantage, stepping between them. Dark eyes stare into mine. My nipples don't understand that Vik is like this with every woman he meets. They perk up at his proximity, super-excited that we have a big, sexy biker spreading our thighs.

Stupid nipples.

"Yesterday you gave me a tattoo," I say suspiciously. "At what point did we discuss becoming roommates?"

He rubs my thigh gently. Frankly, this doesn't seem like roommate behavior. Also? I enjoy it way too much. If we actually shared a place, there's no way I wouldn't jump the man.

"You should relax. You're tense."

"Because you're crazy." Someone clearly has to be the voice of reason here. I'm not sure I'm qualified though because his hand drives me crazy and I'm having serious thoughts about wiggling lower to see if he really is as uninhibited as he seems.

His hand moves higher, and all logical thought vacates my brain. Not only is he crazy, but he cheats.

"Tomato. Tomatoh." He looks supremely unconcerned.

Since I'm right, however, I can't let it go. "We never discussed moving in together."

His hand curls around my thigh. Thank God for denim. It's almost thick enough to allow me to block out the fantastic sensation of those fingers easing up my thigh. Or the other places he could put them. Some of my very *favorite* places.

"You were distracted." His breath ruffles my hair. If he gets any closer, he'll either be in my lap or we'll be simulating sex in public. A quick glance around the clubhouse tells me that no one will notice. There are bikers wrapped around girls, and girls wrapped around various combinations of bikers. It's all very un-PG. People dance, they drink and grind, and apparently they fuck.

In *public*.

I yank my gaze away from the pool table in the corner of the clubhouse. There are things you can't unsee, like the penetration occurring on the green felt surface.

"Yesterday," he says helpfully.

"What about yesterday?"

"I volunteered myself as your booty call. You did not say no."

"Silence isn't a *commitment*." For example, I'm totally thinking about a dozen dirty things he could do with his tongue, but none of those are actual requests.

"You're breathing hard. Are you thinking about me?"

Yes, yes I am.

I deflect. "Are you really that conceited?"

"I'm that good." He slides his hand upward.

I think he's fully prepared to finger me in public. I grab his hand, stopping its upward movement.

"We're in *public*."

"So you'd let me touch if we were alone?" He leans in, his mouth brushing my ear. "Good to know."

"No."

He winks. "I'm even better than your imagination. Let me show you. I make the best friend with benefits."

"Vik—"

"My benefits are huge."

"We are not friends with benefits," I say firmly. I need to get out of here before I forget that and launch myself at him. Stupid body wanting its own personal biker toy. I'm ready for my forever man and happily-ever-after, not a fun diversion. I have my life all mapped out and there's no pit stop for Viking pillaging.

"Maybe I inked my number on your ass last night after you expressed your interest in me." He picks up my hand, running strong thumbs over my palm. With each pass, I melt further.

"You told me you were giving me a firebird."

OMG. He didn't, did he?

"Shhh." He keeps a gentle hold on my hand, turning my arm in his grip. From somewhere he magically produces a Sharpie and uncaps it with his teeth. We both lean in, our heads almost touching, as he scrawls a phone number over my skin.

"Something important?"

He draws the Sharpie down my arm. "Mine."

The possessive note in his voice really demands some kind of response. He doesn't let go of my arm, either. Instead, he starts drawing. Roses and vines. Big, bold flowers. I may never wash again.

"Am I your Etch-a-Sketch now?"

"You deserve flowers." He adds another bloom,

smaller and shyer. I'll have to wear a long-sleeved blouse at work this week but I don't want to pull away. Heading straight to Ink Me seems like my best idea. That way I can see Vik's flowers in color.

"Is that your number?"

His hand glides down my arm to wrap around my fingers. "Yeah."

"Most people just put numbers in their contacts."

"Good point." He caps the Sharpie, vanishing it back into a pocket, and then holds out a hand. "Phone."

Not giving it to him doesn't even occur to me. I pull it out of my purse and hand it over. And then when he taps the screen and looks at me, I type in my passcode. His arm comes around me and he snaps a picture of us.

"What should I call myself in your contacts?" He bends his head over my phone, fingers flying. I didn't know adding a contact was such a multistep process, but whatever. I like watching him. Beautiful doesn't cover it.

"Vik," I say, and he makes a face.

"I should have one of those couples' nicknames. Like peaches or love muffin or big daddy. Christen me now."

The giggle flies out of my mouth like some kind of freakish exploding alien baby. I don't giggle. I'm a mature woman with a career, responsible for millions of dollars of other people's money.

I expect him to give the phone back. He doesn't.

He starts snapping pictures of other bikers, adding them to my contacts list.

"I'm curious, Vik. What am I going to need them for? Body disposal?"

He shrugs and slips my phone back into my purse. "Do whatever needs doing. My old man is gonna love you, though. Can't wait for you to meet him."

Say. What?

"That sounds like a pretty big step."

He presses a kiss against the black rose he's drawn on my skin. "When you know, you know, right? And we've got something, babe."

I reluctantly extricate my arm from his hold. I really shouldn't let the crazy man fondle me, no matter how good it feels. "I'm sure your dad's a lovely man."

Vik purses his lips. "He can be difficult."

"So he's related to you," I say drily.

Vik beams. "And he really, really wants me to settle down. It was kinda a surprise to me. We hadn't talked in months, and then boom. He moves in with me because he's lost his place and now he's after me to find The One. I'm not big on planning, though, so we're taking it one day at a time."

I have no answer—just lots of questions. I start with the obvious. "The One?"

Vik hums a few bars of Mendelssohn's "Wedding March." Most guys aren't big on settling down. I know this thanks to years of looking. Vik, however, looks amused rather than spooked.

"I don't look good in white," he confides. "And the jury's out on diamonds."

Ooookay. Next question.

"You didn't speak? And now he's *living* with you?"

We normal people plunge into family life a little more cautiously. Vik, however, apparently believes in doing everything at Mach Seven.

"I'm turning over a new leaf. Gonna need a new biker name." His smile gets more mischievous, and my panties get correspondingly wetter. "The Saint."

"Excuse me?"

"I'll go by The Saint." He practically bounces on his seat. Unless it's opposite day, this man is about as far from sainthood as you can get.

Since there's no point in disabusing him, I nod amicably. "That's sweet of you."

I haven't met too many people who'd just up and move their dad in because he needed a place. Most people would just toss some cash at the problem— or ignore it. It's a little embarrassing how smiley his protectiveness makes me feel. God, I'm so screwed here. There's all this sexual tension between us and while I know it's as temporary as a firefly, it feels good. Vik's fun and he makes me feel fun. He's just drunk and horny, a biker who does God knows what when he's not inking equally drunk girls. I've never had so much as a speeding ticket.

"I have to go," I say, sliding off the barstool. Staying any longer would be stupid. I've come, I've seen and I've conquered the biker party. I can check one more wild thing off my bucket list.

Vik snags my hand, his fingers rubbing the sensitive skin of my inner wrist. "Already?"

"Yes." That sounds firm. That sounds like a woman who's in charge of her life and the new direction it's taken. Hanging out here any longer would be like trying to make a meal out of cotton candy at the fair. By the time you'd eaten enough to feel full, you'd be sick. Vik is pure sweet evil, and I need to be smart enough to walk away.

"Walk you out" is all he says before getting to his feet. His free hand skims my cheek before falling away, while the fingers braceleting my wrist slide down and tangle with mine until we're holding hands. I take a moment to process that.

He prowls toward the door, which seems about as distant and as unattainable as the peak of the Himalayas. Every fourth step or so some new girl seems to detach herself from the dancing, drinking crowd and tries to attach herself to Vik. It's yet more proof of why any attraction between us is doomed. No matter how pretty he is, I'm not into sharing. I'm more ménage à moi than ménage à trois. The girls climb him like a vine, rubbing and grinding and doing a million other sexy, dirty things I've never done even in the privacy of my own place. It's both impressive and off-putting. Eventually, however, we make it to the door, where he shakes off a final admirer wearing an electric blue tube top as a dress.

He doesn't apologize or acknowledge all the girls hanging on him. It's possible he hasn't even noticed them, that accessories with boobs and vaginas are just that common in the Vik-verse. Yuck. I step outside and inhale a clean, fresh, perfume- and skank-free

breath of air. Kissing Vik would be like making out
with hundreds of other people thanks to his probable
man-whore status.

So I'm passing, no matter how pretty his package is. I lean up, press a kiss against his cheek because I'm weak enough to want that much contact,
and step away.

"Thanks. Tonight was fun."

I'm moving toward my car before I've finished
speaking, just in case Vik has other ideas. Because
well-used or not, I won't stand firm if he puts that
mouth of his to good use. His fingers. His pretty,
pretty...package. Yes, I sneak one last look at the
impressive bulge in his jeans as I hightail it away.
It's like taking a final peep at the Grand Canyon or
some other natural wonder. How can you not look?

He raises a hand, looking amused. "Later."

Oh, I hope not.

Don't I?

CHAPTER SIX

Vik

I WAKE UP way too early for a Sunday morning. We had one hell of a party out at the clubhouse. Fun times. When I was twenty-one and wet behind the ears, it was about the booze and the babes, tapping the ass I could and generally showing life my middle finger. I don't like to plan shit out, but now it's about hanging with my brothers, celebrating another day on the road, another milestone, remembering the good times and not forgetting the bad. On Friday, Hun had officially beaten the charges against him and we'd all raised a beer to that.

I've known plenty of bikers, and we all have stories behind our road names. Some stories are funny, others less so, but I've never figured Hun's out. Depending on his mood, he'll give a dozen different reasons for his label, but they boil down to one of two things. Either he fights with the cunning intensity of a Hun, or he possesses legendary aftercare skills with the club's female hangers-on. He claims the ladies nicknamed him Hon', Honey Bunny or Honey Bunches of Oats because he's that goddamned sweet to them. Most of the brothers just take turns punching him when he says shit like that.

Last night, though, was good. Hun walked free, and we celebrated. Party time's not about knocking back the beer and tequila anymore. Life gets all too real, too fast, so it's important to slow down and savor the good moments. Harper is definitely shaping up to be one of those.

Or if I'm a lucky bastard, a really bad, downright filthy moment. No matter what my old man wants, I'm not a long-term man. He'd like me to find an old lady and settle down, but that's not happening. I don't look past the next weekend, although for Harper I might make an exception and give her more than a night or two. She'd be worth at least a week.

I get out of bed before I can do something really stupid like jerk off to a very fucking fond memory of Harper's heels. Black, leather and a bow tie. Those are the ultimate cock tease in shoes and I'm not dead. I love the way she owns her height. Those four-inch heels scream I can measure up or not. She can take me, leave me, do me—*if* I'm man enough.

My dad's parked in the living room in his boxers, watching *Oprah* reruns and eating toaster waffles. I take a better look at the plate he's holding and revise that to syrup with waffles. I need one of those services that ships meals in a box. Or maybe a breakfast place that delivers. Even fruit would be a step in the right direction. That much Mrs. Butterworth's can't be good for his arteries. Fuck if I know anything about taking care of an old man, but I'll learn.

My old man's not perfect, and neither am I. Between him and the club brothers who patched me in, they kicked my ass into a man who I can mostly face in the mirror. My old man's crotchety and he has a sweet tooth—the rest of him is blunt as fuck. Own up to your mistakes and raise a beer to the successes. That's what he taught me, so now that he needs me to be more, I just have to figure it out.

I give him the side-eye as he waves his sticky fork at me in greeting. "Morning."

It would be better if I'd been waking up with Harper by my side. Or underneath me. On top of me. I'm not picky about her position as long as she's naked and screaming my name.

I grunt a greeting in my old man's direction and grab for the coffeepot. After sex, riding and ink, coffee comes next. Some people fantasize about banging on a beach in Fiji, but I've always thought I'd like to give a coffee plantation in Kona a whirl. Wonder if Harper would be up for that?

I resist the thought and stagger back to the kitchen table. "You have a good night?"

He beams. "Played poker with Lora."

Lora's awesome. She sits with my dad when I go out. She's assured me that she's okay with his incessant flirting, and she also does her best to make sure he's fed and safe. She's a good woman, and I don't need my dad cleaning her out.

"You shouldn't take her money." I empty the coffee as fast as I can. It tastes better than the beers I knocked back last night.

"Won two socks, a flip-flop and her bra." My old man cackles like a maniac. "She refused to ante up her panties."

Jesus.

"But she cleaned out that young man you stuck in the hallway." My old man shoots me a sidelong look.

"Goolie?" Goolie's only been prospecting with us for a month. He did two tours in the Middle East and has a strong preference for not shooting shit anymore.

My old man cackles. "She had him down to his boxers in minutes. Think the bra might have been a decoy." He shakes his head. "She's an awesome fucking woman, and that boy didn't know what hit him. She liked the tattoo on his ass, by the way. Told her that was all your work."

If Goolie up and quits the club, Prez will kick my ass. Babysitting my dad isn't club business, but I cleared it with Prez because I'm not taking chances. Not with my dad's safety. I'm new to this whole responsibility thing but I've already learned that old men can get up to more trouble than teenage boys. That, or he's aiming for payback for the shit I pulled in high school. With interest.

Back then life seemed so simple. You drank, you raced, you thanked God for any girl who'd let you get between her legs and worship her on your knees. And yet somehow all those girls have blurred together, and I've forgotten the shot I had at Harper. She's pretty fucking memorable, so clearly this is on me.

Might be a way to see Harper and take care of some family business, too. I have to fix my old man's finances whether he likes it or not. He's been resisting but he needs to know how much he has, and I need to know how I can add to it so he never goes without.

Too bad if that makes him grumpy.

Fuck that noise.

I go into the kitchen and come back with a glass of orange juice. The carton promises it's full of important vitamins and calcium (which might be another vitamin for all I know about nutrition).

I set the glass in front of him. "I'm making us an appointment with a financial planner."

I wait for the heavens to shoot down lightning at the thought of me planning. Nothing. My dad's interest in Oprah, on the other hand, becomes downright fixated. "That so?"

"Yeah."

"Better be discussing your own stuff. I'm good. I don't need anyone poking around my checking account."

We've had this conversation or a variation thereof ever since my dad showed back up out of the blue a month ago. A social worker called and told me to come and pick him up from the Happy Vegas Valley Trailer Park. He couldn't live alone anymore, the chipper voice on the other end announced. I should have noticed this before but our interactions had been limited to my monthly rides out to his neck of the woods, a little barbecue and a little shooting the breeze. Had to confiscate the keys to his bike, too.

Life's problems have three sure fixes: money, kisses or muscle. Options B and C haven't worked out so well in the taking-care-of-Dad department. And while I have enough green stuff to make sure my old man never goes without, money's not all dear old Dad wants. Dad wants to see me settled. Happy. Set for life. The fuck?

Sure enough, my old man launches into his favorite song.

"You meet anyone last night?"

Seriously, does he think an MC party is Tinder central? Harper came out, I danced and a good time was had by all, but no, I'm not dating anyone.

When I tell him as much, he tries again. "You should see someone. Settle a down a little."

"Like you did with Mom?"

This is a low blow, because Mommy Dearest lit out shortly after my birth and never returned.

"You could get it right," he says stubbornly. "What about Amanda What's-Her-Name? Was she there?"

"Nope." Occasionally I throw my dad a bone and name names. Instead of getting him off my back, however, he's turned out to be downright tenacious. He asks after Amanda (and Hope, Janey and Little Bo) every chance he gets. I've learned to nod, smile and change the fucking topic.

Now is the perfect time to zone out and refresh my memory about my favorite parts of Harper. Tits, ass, mouth—there are so many choices.

"You met someone," my dad announces gleefully. "I know that look."

Busted.

"I'm not looking for anything permanent." I'm good for a night, not forever. Just like that, though, last night's memories of Harper pop into my head and refuse to leave. The memories want to stick even if I don't. Those black boots of hers about killed me. The woman practically owes me mouth-to-mouth resuscitation. Or possibly mouth-to-dick. I'm not choosy.

"Thinks he's fine running solo," my old man scoffs. I'm tempted to point out that *he* never settled down much, either. From what he told me, he knocked up my mom, she stuck around just long enough to push me out into the world, and then she took off. Nothing in that story qualifies him to offer romantic advice.

"I'm not the settling-down type," I offer. That sounds so much better than announcing I like variety in my pussy. And that so far, life has been one big all-I-can-eat sex buffet. Why eat à la carte when I can sample every single dish?

My dad's knee starts going up and down like a jackhammer as he picks up his fork. Sets it down. Does the same with his knife. He starts to get up and then sinks back into his chair, his knee jerking wildly. Shit.

Houston, we have a problem.

The doctor I talked with last week said the agitation was a symptom of my old man's dementia. Much of the time, he's still the same person he always was, but other times his brain takes a hard right and it's game over. The doctor said I should make sure that all of his basic needs are met, as if I'd put him on a starvation diet or keep him from sleeping. I'm supposed to be calm and reassuring, a paragon of gentle sincerity.

Yeah. Feel free to laugh your ass off at that one.

As desperate as I am, though, I try. Thank Christ, none of the club is here to see me.

"I'll give it a shot," I say. "I *am* giving it a shot."

My dad's knee slows from its manic pace to something that better resembles a car ricocheting from side to side on the German Autobahn.

"You've met someone?"

"Absolutely." The one upside to dementia is that my old man's bullshit radar no longer functions.

But he nods, his attention slowly returning to the waffles swimming in a sea of syrup. "I'd like to meet her."

"Soon," I promise. "It's early days. I don't want to scare her off."

He flashes me the bird, but we're back on terra firma. There has to be a way to fix this. Without, you know, actually settling down and paying a trip to the drive-through Elvis wedding chapel on the Strip. Sure, one of the club girls would be happy to pretend to be my steady girlfriend, but I don't think that's what my old man has in mind.

I'll just have to improvise.

Harper's face flashes through my head.

As I fix my own plate of waffles—my old man's onto something there and he's definitely getting a waffle-maker for Christmas—I wonder how an investment banker would feel about becoming a biker's pretend girlfriend. I wonder, too, how long she's spent thinking about my booty call offer. Which was 100 percent fucking genuine. I just need to close the deal. Make her see that I'm the perfect guy to scratch all her itches and give her a little under-the-table loving to help her get over the Douche and on with her life. I'm not boyfriend material, but I'm the Santa Claus of fucking orgasms.

You think she's more likely to kick me in the balls? Good thing I've always loved a challenge.

CHAPTER SEVEN

Harper

WORK IS CRAZY. I stay late each night, retreating back to my Bellagio room with a Subway sandwich or a bag of Mickey D's. It's not even tax season when people get super-concerned about their finances. Yeah, I know they're just looking for a sweet investment to pull in money hand over fist and simultaneously score them some big-ass deduction with the IRS, but their fees keep me employed. And since I only get one chance to make my numbers and impress my bosses, I'm flat-out.

It's not until Thursday night that I return to my old place. Not worrying about Bing is a challenge, but it's not like Mark won't feed him. Plus, even if Mark did forget, Bing would just make Mark's life hell until my ex served up the Fancy Feast. It's no worse than leaving Bing with the cat sitter for company, even if Bing sulks for a week after I've been gone.

Step one in my Break, Enter, Retrieve plan? Getting through the front door. I've banked on Mark's pathological unwillingness to do any household task that he can outsource, and sure enough, he hasn't gotten around to getting a locksmith in. My key still works. There's also no sign of Mark as I open the front door. I breathe a sigh of relief and move on to the second step in the plan. *Retrieve.* Bing likes to hide under our bed, so I scoot up the stairs, cat carrier in hand.

I push the door to the master bedroom open slowly, not wanting to scare Bing. This is a well-executed plan step. The cat doesn't startle.

Hell, no.

I'm the one who freezes in place, peering through the stupid, cracked door.

Turns out, Mark's home after all.

He's eagerly eating out some hussy while she swallows his dick. No. Check that. The woman contorting herself all over my ex is one of Mark's coworkers. The one he used to text and call so often because she had a lousy home situation and lousier husband. They shared a couple of projects. Went out on a few work dinners. Do you hear that sound? It's my rose-colored glasses splintering into a thousand pieces. Fuck me for not recognizing a lie when I heard it. That, or sixty-nine is the new prescription drug for lousy relationships.

The porno moans start up as they round into the home stretch. With each up-and-down, Mark's new friend is practically nose to whiskers with Bing. Bing's eighteen pounds of brown-and-white Siamese love, and he could probably smother that bitch if he sat on her face. Or go to town on Mark's favorite body part. Maybe if I look away, these new-to-me blood-thirsty urges will subside.

Or not.

Mark's replaced me already.

The logical part of my brain (the part not running the odds of a murder conviction if I kill them both now) suggests this might not be the first time Mark's hooked up with his new girl. There's certainly an un-precedented degree of familiarity happening in that bed. Mark's dress pants are unbuckled and shoved down his thighs. Her panties are yanked to the side as if she's so fucking amazing that Mark couldn't wait to undress her. Or maybe he's lazy. God knows, he's never put this much effort into our bedroom time.

The happy twosome shifts and I retreat because I can't handle a close-up of competitor beaver right now. It's not that I want Mark back (especially now I've seen firsthand where he's stuck his dick and his mouth), but I feel like the loser in a race I didn't real-ize I was running. Before I abandon the field to the lucky winner, however, I whip out my phone and snap a couple of pictures. This is immature, but fuck it.

I keep it together as I park my car in the Bellagio's parking garage. I don't break down in the elevator up to my room, and I don't cry the entire, endless length of the hallway. Mark sucks. He's a stupid, cheating, lying bastard and I'm so much better off without him.

Screw him.

No, wait. He's already got that well in hand. Or mouth. Not only is the hussy's beaver now burned into my brain, but I still don't have my cat. I miss Bing, but what if he decides to cozy up to the new body in the bed? What if my cat falls in love with *her*, too?

I strip down to my panties and shimmy into my Kate Spade sleepshirt. Yes, I'm a big believer in brand loyalty. The shirt is black and has cute little white cuffs that make it the comfortable version of one of the many dress blouses I wear to the office—except for the happy fact that my boobs announce *Eat Cake for Breakfast*. I 100 percent endorse that message. I'm giving serious consideration to room-service-ordering up an entire cake.

The Bellagio's bathroom has more mirrors than a voyeur's bedroom, so it's impossible to turn around without catching a glimpse of myself. The funny thing is I look the same, except with bonus red eyes and blotchy cheeks. Sucks to feel different on the inside where no one can see.

The only thing different on the outside is my new ink. I scootch up to the mirror, hike my shirt up under my armpits in the least sexy move ever and ease my panties halfway down my butt. And then I'm staring at my lower back and ass. You know, just checking shit out.

Even with the tattoo only half-healed, it's clear that Vik is insanely talented with his hands. My firebird explodes up from the base of my spine, wings expanding from my panties and wrapping themselves around my spine. The feathers are this gorgeous red and black, long, sweeping lines of color that soar upward. For all his teasing, Vik didn't ink his number on my butt.

Okay. So he didn't give me his number in permanent color but he's still beneath my skin. There's all that bare skin around the lines he laid down, just begging to be filled. I want more, want that darkness, that sweet pain and the release that comes afterward. The buzz of his needle let me forget so much and then took me to a different place.

I pick up my abandoned clothes. Fold them neatly and stack them on the opulent little vanity bench. The Bellagio has its King Louis the Something-Something going on because my bathroom is practically raining gilt. My black work skirt and Kate Spade blouse look downright sedate, and my beige bra is the cherry on the boring sundae. To be fair, it's not like I can rock red lace underneath a white work blouse, nor do I want to, but still…my underwear covers more than most bikinis. If I got hit by a bus and EMTs stripped me down to check for injuries, my modesty would be safe.

Mark's hussy wore red satin.

I promptly Google selfie tips.

I must be crazy because I'm actually thinking about taking a picture. Of my panties. I recheck the all-knowing Internet, and three minutes later I'm armed, dangerous and pointing my phone at my crotch. Snap, snap, tap. It's not even hard. Sure, I hesitate, my finger hovering over Vik's contact info. For like a nanosecond.

I hit Send. Are these panties boring?

Is sharing mostly naked selfies with an almost total stranger stupid?

Yes.

Yes, it is.

And then, still feeling reckless, I march out and raid the minibar. Never mind that the smallest package of M&M's costs a ridiculous eight dollars or that the price tag on the mini champagne exceeds my last cell phone bill. I'm totally worth it, and today has sucked.

My phone dings with an incoming message.

VIK: You do have my number. Thought you'd never use it.

ME: Answer the question.

VIK: Would look better on the floor. Or wrapped around my dick. Hint hint.

It's silly to be happy because Vik likes my panties. His opinion is hardly statistically significant— I'd have to march my butt out onto the Strip and poll at least ninety-nine other random guys if I wanted meaningful results. But still. *He* likes beige just fine. Of course, that's because he wants to get *in* them but I totally count it as a win for me.

ME: Tried to pick up my cat from my ex. Epic fail.

VIK: Tell me what you need. I'm on it.

ME: Brain bleach.

He's a biker who goes to biker parties, so a random couple 69-ing won't shock him. I text him my new glamor shot of Mark and his colleague. Frankly, the only reason I'm not blasting it to everyone we know is that then I'd have to explain what I was doing in his house after he gave me the boot.

VIK: I'd say fuck him but looks like he's already got that covered. You can do better than him. I can be there in thirty minutes if you decide to upgrade.

See? I'm sexy.

ME: Flying solo tonight but thanks.

VIK: You sure about that?

ME: Not in the mood for company. Swearing off sex forever.

VIK: Give me a shot.

ME: At?

VIK: Changing your mind. You've had the worst. No point in taking a vow of celibacy until you've tried the best.

ME: So you're the best?

Vik texts me back a row of smiley-face emoticons. I have no idea what that means.

Absolutely none.

Is he in a good mood? Laughing at me? Tapped the wrong picture when he meant to send a chorus line of dancing eggplant emojis?

I consider what I know. Item one? I definitely like his body. New Me has fantasized a lot about stripping him down and licking various parts of his anatomy. But those are just fantasies—and Real Me lives firmly in reality. He's hot, and I'm me. Most days, I'm happy to be me. But I'm a conservative investment banker. I wear panty hose. I plan for the long game. No matter how pretty Vik is, he's not my type.

The line of dancing dots appears on my phone.

VIK: Assuming you're not at work?

ME: Nope. Back at the Bellagio.

Ten long heartbeats later, my phone buzzes.

He's sent me a picture.

If I had to pick a word to describe what I'm looking at, I'd be hard-pressed to choose, but *dirty* vies for top position on my list. The shot closes in on his abs and then goes…lower. Much, much, deliciously lower. He's unbuttoned the top buttons of his jeans and he's fisting his dick. The view is both hot as fuck and supremely frustrating because while I know *where* his hand is (squeezing what appears to be a magnificently large penis), I can't see much of anything. Video would be so much better.

VIK: Sweet dreams.

It's definitely time to sign off. Otherwise, I'll be asking him to come over here and show me his Monster Dick in person.

ME: Again? Covered.

I scoop up my snack pile and then text him a picture of my loot. It's not a sexy look, but I'm nervous about taking the next step with him.

VIK: Looks small. The snack, not your tits ;) Perfect mouthful right there.

ME: Girl's gotta do what a girl's gotta do.

VIK: Hear you.

We sign off, and I sigh with relief. I haven't said or done anything too incriminating, like beg him to come over and express his appreciation for my boobs in person. Since the fountain show is scheduled to go off in five minutes, I camp out by the window. The Bellagio has the best furniture—I seriously want to load it all into my car when I check out and take it with me.

The fountains explode, and I hold up my phone, making a video. I'll bet Vik could come up with a dozen different dirty innuendoes for all that water jetting upward. I'll have to challenge him.

The knock on my door comes just as the fountains shoot their final load sky high. After checking through the peephole to make sure it's not a serial killer (bad) or a wayward biker (bad but oh so good), I open the door and let the room service guy in.

"Got a special delivery for you, Ms. George," he says before I can point out that I haven't ordered anything tonight. "Compliments of a Mr. Vik."

And then bless the man, he wheels in a trolley, whips off a half-dozen silver domes and reveals the entire dessert menu. It's like a multiple choice test where you're supposed to choose which plate of decadent goodness is your favorite, A, B, C, D, or E—all of the above. This is clearly a vote for E.

Guess I do get to have cake for breakfast after all.

CHAPTER EIGHT

Harper

THREE DAYS AFTER the dessert incident, I stagger back into the Bellagio clutching a foot-long sub in a bag. Work sucked the big one, and my evening plans consist of mainlining carbs and greasy sandwich meat until I burst. Pepperoni, salami, cheese and banana peppers—what's not to love? Sure, tonight's dinner packs 940 calories and forty-eight grams of fat, but those details are on my to-ignore list for tonight. It would take hours to burn them off on the elliptical machine in the gym downstairs, but I've already decided that they're welcome to take up permanent residence on my hips.

I really need to invest in a place with an actual kitchen, but the last place I looked at was a complete nightmare. The zip code was great, offering a rental in one of those tall, sleek high-rise buildings full of chic condos. New Me liked the white and chrome—it made us feel sexy and sophisticated. Turned out I wasn't the only one feeling the *Fifty Shades of Grey* vibes. From the moaning and thumping echoing through the small space, the neighbors to the left were going at it. The Realtor and I both started giggling so hard that I was afraid I'd interrupt the guy's rhythm.

So now here I am, just me, my sandwich and I. A foot-long dick or margarita sounds like more fun, but I'll have to make do with carbs. When I reach my room, however, the door is ajar on the latch. Since I don't see the housekeeping cart, I ease the door open and peer inside, ready to jump back if there's an assailant hiding in the bathroom.

Nope.

No bad guy—other than the six feet, three inches of biker sprawled on my bed. Vik grins lazily at me as I hover in the doorway.

"You've got four porn channels."

"That cost twenty dollars each."

I step inside and shut the door behind me. I'm not entirely certain what to do or say, but since Vik has made himself at home without an invitation, I figure he has some kind of plan.

"How did you get in? Just out of curiosity?"

He lays his finger beside his nose and winks. "Trade secret, babe. I brought you something. Guess."

I'm sure it's no surprise that I suck at games. "An exercise bike so I can work off some of the calories you had delivered the other night?"

His gaze slides down my body. "We need to be clear on one thing. I don't have to hold back, do I?"

I roll my eyes. "As if you would."

"True." He nods. "So I'm just gonna say that you look amazing. Guess again."

"Flowers." I should be exasperated, but he's so fucking cute. He bounces on the bed, his eyes gleaming with mischief. Whatever his present is, I doubt it's as tame as a florist's bouquet.

He rolls his eyes. "Only roses I do are ink."

He leans over the side of the bed and lifts something up. "Voilà!"

He's brought me a cat carrier. No, *better*. He's brought me *my* cat carrier and that means—

"You stole my cat!" I'm pretty sure I shriek the words, but Bing's already meeping his own hellos and demanding that some human spring him from the carrier *now*. Bing has zero patience and isn't a fan of waiting. If he ever had to live in the wild, he'd starve within a week because he's not the kind of cat that could lay low, stalking its prey for hours on end. Like me, Bing prefers his food hot, tasty and delivered.

"Technicalities. I *sprang* your cat. Set him free. Reunited him with the one love of his life because I'm such a fucking romantic." Vik flops back on the bed dramatically, arms splayed out on either side of him. Whatever point he's trying to make is lost on me because his T-shirt rides up, exposing a chiseled stomach that demands licking.

I err on the side of caution and fly around the side of the bed to spring Bing from prison. Bing's all over me, too, like we've been parted for months and months. He rubs and purrs, and I try to pretend I'm just having an allergic reaction and not tearing up. When a tissue dangles in front of my nose, I take it.

Eventually Bing decides he's had enough of me (or needs to teach me a lesson for abandoning him to Mark's dubious charms) and disappears under the bed to check out his new kingdom. Vik rolls off the bed, saunters over to the table by the window. His butt in those jeans is a work of art. They should showcase it in the fine art gallery downstairs. Better yet, if he were on display, he wouldn't be reaching for my sandwich bag. He pulls my dinner out, unwraps it and takes an enormous bite.

"That's mine."

"I rescued your cat. I don't get a thank-you present?"

"Thank you." I grin happily at him—and stick my hand out for the sandwich. Hello. I haven't had dinner yet.

"Halfsies?" He gives me a charming grin, which is not what I need right now. Hell, now I'm going to have to share with both a biker *and* a cat. I'll be lucky to end up with any sandwich meat at all. It'll be all banana peppers and lettuce for me.

"How did you convince Mark to give up Bing? Wait. Back up." I'm missing a step here. "How did you know where I lived?"

He shrugs like it's no BFD. "You had to give your driver's license to Gia at Ink Me. And Mark the Douche may not be aware that he's a cat light at the moment."

"You stole my cat." I know I've already said this, but it bears repeating.

He hands me half of my sandwich. "That's a technicality. I left the back door wide-open on my way out. Just how much of a dick is your ex?"

Sadly, I don't have to think hard. "Huge. He's a dick of pornographic proportions. Twelve inches of sleazy man schlong."

"Then we're good. He won't want to tell you that he lost your Precious."

I'm not sure what he expects me to say. *Yeah, thanks so much for committing a felony on my behalf. I must be some sort of freak because I find it kind of hot, so maybe we can go knock over a bank or clean out Tiffany's before you ride away?* None of those seem appropriate, so I concentrate on my sandwich.

My *half* a sandwich.

Now that I've got Bing, I'm not giving him back. From the way he's wolfing down salami, I'm not sure Mark was feeding him.

"I can't keep a cat in a hotel room. I don't even have a litter box."

Vik points to the corner. "I brought supplies."

In my reunion glee, I hadn't even noticed the two large carriers from the pet store chain. There's even a giant plastic container of cat litter. I spare a second to wonder how Vik got all this up here. Or if he came on his bike.

"But I've got a better idea." He polishes off his sandwich half and looks hopefully at mine. Not a chance. I shove the rest of it into my mouth, and he snorts. "You don't like to share, do you?"

"Uh…" I work on chewing and swallowing.

"You're in luck, babe. I'm very good at sharing. You and Bing can move in with me."

I choke on the last bite of my sandwich. "You don't think that's a little too friendly? First you offer to be my booty call, and now you're offering to be my roommate?"

"I'll even put out for you." He winks at me. "Total friends with benefits."

"What?" I shake my head, pretending I'm not staring at his chest. He makes it so hard to think straight. "I can't move into some stranger's place. That's like just begging you to be a serial killer and bury me under the porch."

"Don't have a porch, babe. You're safe." He reaches out and tugs me down onto the bed beside him. This is dangerous territory. It's not that Vik doesn't take *no* for answer—it's that I'm all *yes, yes, yes* when I'm around him.

"We barely know each other," I protest.

I sound totally mature, like a grown woman making all the right decisions. Good one, brain. If I'd known he'd be here tonight, I'd have made a list of all the reasons why moving in with him was a really bad idea. In fact, once he leaves tonight, I'll get right on that. And this new plan of mine is totally working, right up until the moment he rolls over and props himself up on one arm. One hard, inked, super-close-to-me arm.

His bare skin is my Waterloo.

Worse, he tugs me closer with his free arm. My stupid, traitorous body rolls right up against him like we fit together. I'm always taller than most of the men I meet. Mark was two inches shorter, although he claimed we were the same height. Vik being built like a mountain, however, almost makes me seem petite. Okay. Not really, but we're a good match.

"I know you're fucking gorgeous." His gaze, full of appreciation, slides over me, and I swear I feel my clothing melting away.

"That's an outside thing, not an inside." I know I'm not making a whole lot of sense but I blame that on *his* outside. He's still way too gorgeous, and whenever I look at him, my brain stops functioning. Plus, now my fingers are sort of petting his arm, tracing the dark swirls of ink that wrap around one hard, perfect male bicep.

Biting him is suddenly way too tempting.

"Inside, huh? Too bad I can't remember our first meeting." He laughs wickedly when I pinch him. Guess he doesn't mind a little pain, either. "I know plenty about you, Harper. I know you like numbers, you count everything, you're way too nice for a guy like me and you're good with animals. Those are all good qualities in a roommate, although your being nice won't stop me from trying to score with you. I'll bet you're also the bomb at paying bills on time and doing all the organizational shit. I should probably be paying you, if we're being honest."

"You're good at this compliment business," I observe.

"You don't believe me?" He rolls and somehow I end up underneath him. This isn't a hardship, particularly when he eases my glasses off my nose and sets them down on the bedside table.

Still, a girl has to have her principles.

"You're a player. I don't think we should be talking about this."

"You don't have anywhere to live. You're looking for a place."

"True." Moving sucks, but getting summarily evicted with zero warning hurts even more. Playing by the rules hasn't won me the prize. I had a master plan and the execution seemed straightforward. Bachelor's degree from an Ivy. Master's from the same. Fill my 401K and my checking account, get a place of my own and conquer the career track before turning thirty. Stay at a prominent investment firm or start my own company—it'll be my choice. I'll find a guy who shares my goals and values and we'll get married. Settle down in our McMansion, discuss whether or not we want our 2.3 kids and when. I thought Mark was that guy, The One, and if he hadn't been my One and Only, he'd have certainly been good enough. Now I have to start all over again.

"So why not live with me?"

"Because it's really freaking hard to find Mr. Right when you're shacking up with...with..."

"Mr. Right Now?" Vik beams at me. "Not a problem."

He has no idea.

I push him up and roll off the bed before I do something really stupid. Such as riding him like a cowgirl. Or reverse cowgirl…yeah. I like that plan. Of course he follows me, putting my strategic retreat at risk.

"You really want to find Mr. Right?"

I stare out the window. The Bellagio has awesome views of the Strip, all blinking, whirring lights and waterworks. If I have to be homeless, this is definitely the place to do it. I shouldn't be whining about being out of a place when I'm here and so many other people are less fortunate.

"I do," I say to my reflection. "I really do. It's what I've been planning."

"And you like your plans." Vik's head nods in the glass. I think he might actually understand, not that it matters. He's not the one in charge of my life or my dreams, although I kind of like hearing that he doesn't think I'm crazy. Not that he's said that, but I'm reading between the lines.

"Being organized is important."

"I'm not looking for any kind of right, Mr. or Ms. I'm not boyfriend material." He plants his hands on either side of me. I could duck. I could go left or right.

I don't.

His mouth finds my ear. "Ask me what I'm good at, Harper."

"Do tell."

"Fuck buddy," he says roughly. "I'm the best toy ever and I don't even need batteries."

The man makes an interesting point. He's not my Mr. Right but since those plans are temporarily on hold...why not seize the moment? We can be friends. Hang out. Explore some sexy side benefits. Maybe he'll even take me for a ride every now and then, and I'll...fuck if I know what I have to offer. I'm solid and stable and way too boring for a man like this.

"You think too much," he says roughly.

"Impossible." I scoot around so I can see his pretty, pretty face because he's even more fun to look at than the Strip.

And then he kisses me, ruining everything.

Vik doesn't kiss me soft, doesn't lead up to the main event. No surprise that he's all in, his mouth taking mine in a hard, thorough kiss as he catches my face in his hands. Heat shoots through me as fast and high as the fountains outside. He knows just how to flip my switch and get me going. Pure animal heat. I've been kissed before but never like this.

I fist his hair, dragging him closer.

I've never wanted anyone more. Or faster. All the hot, painful, pent-up need inside me explodes as I kiss him back. When my knees actually go weak and I sag against him, he chuckles and lifts me like I weigh nothing at all.

"Legs," he whispers against my ear, and I shiver. I do what he says, or try to. His hands bunch beneath my butt, arranging me. Fabric tears because pencil skirts weren't made for man-humping, but do I give a fuck? No, I do not. My legs part around his waist and then I'm grinding against his dick. God, his dick is spectacular. It's as big and thick as every other part of him, and I ride it shamelessly. I don't care that I'm pressed up against the glass, giving the entire Strip a show.

Vik kisses me back like kissing me is the only thing that matters right now. His tongue leaves no inch of me untouched, stroking deep and then light and then who knows what the hell he does but it's so goddamned amazing that I pull at his hair, steering his head in search of more. He hangs on to me like letting go just isn't possible, and I like it. I like him. There's just something about this biker that makes *all* of me weak.

Or to be more specific, his hands *definitely* make me weak. One calloused finger traces the edge of my panties. The big, bad wolf is knock, knock, knocking at my door and I'm ready to beg him to come in and eat me up.

This needs to stop.

But...

He slides a fingertip beneath the lace trim. He's not stopping. He's...

A tease.

Because that finger *does* stop moving, and it takes all the willpower I have not to wiggle until it's right smack on top of my clit. And then I'd have a few directions for him. It wouldn't take long, not the way he has me worked up.

"Test ride," he growls, his mouth so close to mine that I could make him my own personal lollipop and lick him.

"What?" Proximity has short-circuited my brain. "Take me for a test ride as your fuck buddy. Lemme show you what your new best friend can do."

CHAPTER NINE

Vik

HARPER STARES AT me like I've poured Kool-Aid into the Holy Grail and asked her if she was thirsty. Not sure if that's good or bad, but she's listening.

So I give her the truth even though my finger's inches from sinking into her hot, wet heat. Even though I could make her forget everything—my name, her name, the name of the fucking president. Almost kills me to wait.

"I'm sorry I don't remember you," I admit. "Got plenty of excuses but here's the truth. Forgetting is on me, not you. The fault's all mine, and I'd really like to make it up to you."

We're pressed against the window, my hands wrapped around her ass, and I'm begging. She's not just a woman I want to bang. I can't shove her panties aside and drive deep inside her, not without giving something else up. Don't know what it is or what it'll cost me, but I plan on finding out. I'm not kidding about being her fuck buddy. She doesn't want a relationship with me, but sex?

She's definitely gonna want sex with me.

"Give me ten minutes." That's nine minutes more than I need to make her come, but once won't be enough.

Harper looks at me like she's been stuck in a desert without food or water for the last month, and has just stumbled upon a Vegas buffet in an oasis. I'd love to be on her menu tonight, but I need some words from her first. *Yes, Vik* works. As does *Do me now, Vik* or *For the love of God, give me your dick.* I'm not particular.

"Why?" That's not a *no*—I'm almost in. And then she slides her hands around my neck, fingers tangling in my hair. I don't know what I'll do if she tells me to go. If I can't convince her to give me this shot.

"Because I've got a plan," I whisper roughly against her mouth. Harper fucking loves plans. If I whipped out a PowerPoint presentation, she might come on the spot. It's fucking adorable. "You want to hear it?"

"Is it a good plan?" Her fingers tighten and I hold still. Is she pulling me closer or pushing me away?

"It's a bad plan." I nip her bottom lip. "The very best bad plan ever."

Her grip tightens and she pulls my head back until she can meet my gaze full-on. It's fucking amazing.

"I'm sure a million women have told you how beautiful you are." She stares into my eyes, taking inventory. Don't know what she sees there because inside I'm a whole lot of nothing, but she sighs. A soft tease of sound and air that brushes over my mouth in an almost-kiss, reminding me just how close she is.

"I'm not sure you realize that there's more to you

than just your outside," she continues. "You're a good man, even if you try to hide it underneath all that ink and leather."

"I can't be your boyfriend. I won't be your forever man." Pretty sure I fucking growl the words, but her legs are wrapped around my waist and her pussy's riding my dick. I have zero fucking clues as to what she's talking about, and right now I don't care.

"Got it." She sighs. "You're a loaner dick."

And since I don't know what to say to that, I try kisses instead. I lean in, brushing my mouth over hers, licking at her lower lip.

"Harper." There's no way I forget her, not this time, not ever again.

If you've got amnesia, you revisit all your old haunts, right? To see if anything comes back to you? I skim a finger beneath the edge of Harper's panties, waiting for the memories to rush back. I've got nothing, nothing but a hot, slick path leading straight to temptation. Never has a man been more willing to fall. I stroke higher, taking my time because she feels that fucking good. How could I possibly have forgotten this?

"You need to know something," she whispers.

I stop moving, stop fucking breathing. Take my hand back. If she needs me to listen, that's what I'll do. "Hit me."

"This is just sex, and that's perfect, but I've never been big on one-night stands or quickies so I'm a little out of my league here and I don't want to disappoint.

Also? Seeing as how you're the hottest man I've ever known, I'm a little nervous about doing—"

"Shhhh." I brush my mouth over hers. "Anyone ends up disappointed tonight, it's my fault."

"Are you shushing me?"

"You want to talk afterward, I'm all yours. Give you at least nine minutes then, but this time is mine." I nip her lower lip, leaving the sweetest, pinkest mark.

"I'm timing you," she says breathlessly.

Her phone's halfway across the room, so unless she can count and come at the same time, I'm safe. Just to be sure, I ease my hand up her leg again, curving my fingers around her butt and then sinking lower for gold. I stroke the soft silky fabric of her panties. Christ, she's so wet that I can feel it.

"This is step one in my plan." I drag my fingers up the seam of her slit, circling her clit. She's been so good that she deserves a reward. Or I do. Fuck if I care if it means I get to touch her. "You got any feedback for me, babe?"

And then I kiss her before she can answer me, because it's easier for her to let go and get lost in the pleasure if she's not talking. Plus, I really love kissing her. I slide my mouth hard against hers until she opens up and lets me all the way in.

She tastes so much better than I imagined.

She tastes sweet and ripe as she comes undone for me, and I pull her closer, wanting everything. Her thighs tighten on my waist and she moans. It's not enough. I slide my fingers beneath the edge of her panties, move them over slick, wet pussy. She's fucking juicy. I need to lick her clean, then make her dirty all over again.

"Vik." She whimpers my name, making that one word into a plea. Yeah. I'll give her what she wants. I'm all hers.

"Step two. Gonna owe you some new panties. Take you shopping tomorrow if you want."

I don't wait for her nod—the cream slicking my fingers is all the permission I need. I tear that tiny tease of a panty off her and drop it onto the floor. We don't need anything between us. I circle her clit.

And then she loses it, which has to be the fucking dirtiest, most beautiful thing I've ever seen. She arches against me, bucking and grinding against my dick because now she's taking what she wants, and I can come along for the ride or not. I want to fuck her on the floor, on the back of my bike, down on the Strip in the fountain in full view of the entire world because this woman...

Harper.

She's everything to me.

Just for right now, just for tonight because fuck buddies don't last, but she's the most beautiful woman I've ever seen and she makes me feel like she sees me the same way I do her. I push a finger into her hard, and she takes it. She takes the next one, too, both of us leaning apart so we can see where we're joined together, my fingers stretching her obscenely wide.

Christ, she's tiny. It's gonna be a rough, hard ride.

She's close. Her pussy tightens on my fingers, squeezing hard, and I need to get my dick in her now. I'll give her all the orgasms in the world later tonight, but I have to be inside her this first time. Just to be certain, though, I press the pad of my finger against her G-spot. Her face scrunches up in an almost-frown, her body stilling.

"Vik—"

Gotta love the way she moans my name. I know lots of women believe the G-spot's either a myth or an optional accessory not all of you come with, but I'm a master hunter and I find what I'm looking for. I curl my fingers like I'm trying to stroke her from the inside out, and she loses it. She starts babbling something about seeing stars and she's not even looking at the goddamned sky.

She's looking at *me*.

I unbuckle and unbutton, shoving my jeans down just enough to get free and get a condom out, pressing Harper against the window with one hand and my weight. As if she'd go anywhere now. As if I could let her go. I don't care if the Four Horsemen of the Apocalypse come down from heaven promising orgasms and a million bucks, I'm not stepping aside. Not now.

"Ask me." I know my voice sounds hard and mean but I need her to give me this much. "Tell me to give it to you, Harper. Tell me you want this."

"I want you," she pants out as I roll on the condom. Thank fuck.

I lift her up, bring her down and give it to her good.

CHAPTER TEN

Harper

THE RETURN TO consciousness is slow. In fact, if it wasn't for the cold glass pressed against my naked butt, I'd stay happily comatose for the next century or so. Unless, you know, Vik has plans for a repeat. I could probably, maybe bestir myself for another epic orgasm.

I bury my face in his neck and zone out for a blissful moment. He mutters something creatively obscene, and then he lifts me off his fantastic dick, cradling me against his chest. My back hits the mattress, but I hang on tighter to my man pillow. As awesome as the Bellagio's four-hundred-count sheets are, Vik's chest is better.

"Should I go? Or can I have ten more minutes?" The mattress dips as Vik follows me down. Not that I'm giving the man much choice—I'm attached tighter than a monkey to a banana.

"Can't," I mumble. "Need some time to recuperate, 'kay?"

He chuckles, a dirty sound that rumbles through my cheek (because I'm still pressed against him) and then down lower. I'm humming and thrumming all over, but particularly in my lady parts. Who knew I could come so hard? Checking the time is low down on my priority list, but I have a sneaking suspicion the man didn't even need the full nine minutes to make fireworks go off in my body.

"Can I recuperate with you?" He rolls us over smoothly, tucking a pillow beneath my cheek. My back's pressed against his front, his arm wrapped around my waist. I spare half a second to wonder where our clothes and the used condom went and then decide I don't care.

"Be my guest," I wriggle backward, getting comfortable. He groans, and things start getting interesting. Too bad for him that he wore me out with his super dick. My last conscious thought is that booty calls rock.

Vik slips away sometime between giving me an epic orgasm and sunrise. Not only does he feed Bing on his way out, but he draws me a note on the pet food receipt—a stick man with an enormous penis waving goodbye. So when he texts me later that morning, I answer. And then he replies, and somehow we fall into a routine of texting.

And it's not just sexy talk, although that part's great. Two mornings after our magnificent bang fest, I ask him what he's working on. I'm up to my eyeballs in client folders, juggling numbers, and I need a break. He takes so long to answer that I decide I've scared him off. Maybe dicks and the activities of said dicks are the only acceptable topics of conversation in the Vik-verse, but it seems weird to me. And then he responds. With a picture. A dozen blackbirds fly free from the tip of a black feather that's all thick, dark lines and shadows. "Take flight, my brother" is sketched beneath the flying birds, and then a pair of dates. I can just see the edges of Vik's rough, beat-up fingers in the shot. It's freaking amazing, but it's also sad and wild and those birds... Vik's birds are going places, and both the journey and the destination seem like they'd be worthwhile.

ME: Who did you lose?

VIK: Ink's for one of my brothers. We like to think Bingo's just riding on ahead scouting. Gonna catch up with him someday.

Sometimes you have to let people go. We both know this. And sometimes...maybe sometimes they're not gone—just riding up ahead and out of sight, and someday you'll turn the corner and catch up. I like the thought of that.

He wants to know what my day looks like, so I send him a selfie of me making crazed eyeballs over an enormous stack of file folders. He offers to swing by my office and help me clear off that desk; I counter by telling him that you have to have an appointment to get anywhere near my...desk.

He likes that.

After that, we just keep texting. Weeks pass like this and in the meantime, I pack up my suite at the Bellagio and move into my newly leased condo—getting Bing back forced me find something quick.

I know Vik and I are just friends with benefits, but apparently one of the unexpected benefits is having someone to talk to. *With*. Because Vik listens and he asks questions and…

Yeah. I don't know what I'm thinking, either.

We had wild, crazy, onetime, up-against-a-window sex, and I liked that. Okay. I freaking loved it, but I'm currently pretending that we absolutely didn't do something so publicly dirty. Or that I kind of want to do it again with my new friend. In fact, thinking about the awesome sex I had two weeks ago with Vik is what makes me late for work this morning. I've never mastered the fine art of jilling in the shower. Balancing and rubbing on all that tile in my new place isn't my strong point, so when the urge to rub one out gets too strong to ignore, I head back to bed.

I slide between the sheets, shove my fingers between my legs and start up a go-to fantasy in my head. I'm backstage at a concert, and the band's just coming offstage. They're all big and sweaty, adrenaline and power rolling off them because they know they've got an entire crowd at their feet and they fucking love it. But then the lead singer spots me waiting by the side of the stage and he beckons me over. We don't make it to the green room. He just yanks up my skirt and tears open his jeans, and then he's slamming into me and we're perfect together. The rest of the band is watching or walking on, and I know other crew members and groupies can see us. But the singer's mine.

I look up and realize it's no singer. It's Vik pounding into me hard, his eyes watching mine as he gives me what I want. And I'm right there, teetering on the brink of a motherfucking huge orgasm, my thighs and my butt tensing as I ride my fingers straight toward the almighty finish line. Faster and faster, my fingers rubbing and circling right where I need him the most, and then what seems like the entire motorcycle club suddenly surrounds us, a band of brothers dedicated to lending a helping hand, and I come so hard that I see stars.

So I'm more than a little out of breath after finishing my ménage à moi. My new condo is also farther from my office than before, and I'm still getting used to traffic. It's a one-bedroom tucked into a new highrise. The walls are white, the carpet's white, even the appliances are a gleaming stainless steel. I feel like I've landed inside an igloo or some chic pied-à-terre in Antarctica—and I like it. It's a fresh start while I figure out who I am now.

Which is late. Very, very, inexcusably late. So late that I have to sprint from the parking garage to the elevator. Eighteen floors are barely enough to suck in some air and check my buttons and seams in the elevator mirrors. No woman wants to walk into her office with her skirt tucked into her panties.

Even if it is a really good skirt. My Dolce & Gabbana

skirt hugs my butt and hips before flaring out over my knees. They make skirts in crazy prints like pineapples, fish and cabbage roses, but this one is a perfectly sensible, entirely professional black. The little black bow at the throat of my Kate Spade blouse is as much fun as I had when I got dressed today. Who's going to trust his bankroll to a woman wearing pineapples on her skirt?

I inhale, exhale. Today's going to be a great day. I've got this. The door dings open softly as I finish my affirmation. I love our office, and not just because it has the kind of steel-and-chrome good looks that star in architectural porn. Money has a smell. On a good day when the market's playing out how we predicted, we practically print that shit here. On a bad day, the senior partners scream at their junior mini-mes and head downtown to drown their woes. Being able to hold your alcohol is a requirement for scoring a corner office and a seat with the big boys, as is an advanced degree in bullshitting and spotting a market trend and riding that big boy straight into the money.

Finance is still very much a boy's world. Like a handful of women, I've muscled my way in and I'm allowed to stay as long as I bring in the green, but despite the ubiquitous presence of both a boys' and a girls' bathroom, finance is a male sandbox. It's just that possessing a vagina instead of a dick is no longer an automatic bar to entry.

Margie intercepts me as soon as I step off the elevator. My usually calm assistant looks flustered. "Your eight o'clock is here."

Rewind.

I had an *eight* o'clock?

Margie makes an apologetic face. "He called and scheduled last minute, so he wasn't on your calendar. He needs to go over his dad's finances and heard you were the best."

He's right but even I need some prep time.

"Give me five minutes and then show him in," I say. "Hit him with coffee and doughnuts or something. A nice bran muffin, courtesy of the house."

No matter how much money they have, people always like free food, and Margie's a goddess at smoothing ruffled feathers. If the newest client on the block is upset by starting at 8:06, she'll fix it. I grab the folder Margie holds out to me. Usually, Margie would enter the client's information into our system, but since he's a last-minute appointment, she hasn't had the chance.

I park at my desk and start flipping through the papers. Jeez. The client's reason for arriving in my office before eight in the morning is painfully clear. The father has some kind of military pension, an annuity, significant gambling winnings and a less lucrative penchant for day-trading. Oh, and a trailer in a park about a hundred miles outside Vegas—not exactly waterfront property.

Margie buzzes, our signal that I should come collect my new clients. Brain working overtime, I head out.

And stop short.

Margie doesn't notice I'm flustered because her own cheeks are pink. Vik has that effect on women.

"Mr. Ash Ilin and Mr. Serge Ilin," Margie says as if she's announcing the King and Queen of England. I practically hear trumpets and a twenty-one-gun salute.

Instead of a crown, Vik carries a cup of coffee. I wonder if the man has ever worn a suit. Bet if he got married, he'd hit the church in jeans and leather. Beside him, an older, more wrinkled and weather-beaten version clutches an enormous stack of dough-nuts wrapped in a napkin.

"Thanks, darling." Vik gives Margie a big smile and she beams back like they've been best friends since the second grade. His gaze shifts to me.

Shoot.

That one-night fuck buddy thing we had? I don't think it's over. Completely inappropriate, not-safe-for-work heat stabs through me. And it's a total waste because whatever brought Vik here, it's not me. He's not jonesing for a repeat of our booty call, and what-ever he wants from me, it's not a relationship. The man's a man whore, candy of the best kind, and I am officially on a diet.

Starting now.

Maybe I didn't make our onetime status clear. Maybe all the screaming and oh-God-more-now-please confused him. But he's super-cute with his dad.

"What are you doing here?"

"Financial things," he says cheerfully, and tips his head at the old guy by his side. "This is my dad."

Introductions are made, and I can't help but notice that Vik's father checks me out very, very carefully.

Not in a creepy way, but as if he's interested in more than my financial planning skills. He beams at me when he shakes my hand, declaring that he's thrilled to finally meet me.

Finally?

I turn back to Vik. "I'm still confused as to why you're *here*."

Vik winks. "I'm your eight o'clock."

When I said he needed an appointment to get into my...office, I was only playing.

Mostly.

The only thing worse than having a secret crush on a badass biker is having that same biker show up at your office on a Monday morning. Just in time... wait for it...for all the senior partners to walk past on their way to their weekly meeting. The suit parade slows to take inventory. Our clients come in all shapes, sizes and colors, and there's no dress code. Honestly, the only thing that matters is the size of your bank account and your willingness to let us play with it. But even so, Vik sticks out.

Polite surprise is etched across their sober faces. And while I know some of them cut up on their downtime, once they're in the office, it's game time. Our minimum requirement for doing business is usually a cool million—and Vik's dad has a trailer and a military pension. Unless said trailer is parked on top of a massive oil well or perhaps a diamond mine, I'm not sure how I can help—but I want to.

Vik rocks back on his heels—heels in well-worn leather motorcycle boots—and nods agreeably at the parade. He looks every inch the badass biker (except for the little old man accessory that he clearly cares about) and I can feel disapproval from my coworkers and bosses. Or maybe I'm just projecting.

"Let's go into my office and hash this out." I lead the way, pretending I can't feel Vik's gaze checking out my butt.

My office isn't a corner office—not yet—but it's nice. I've got a big black power desk and a pair of expensive black leather sofas. And since I like a little color, I've got a matching set of modern art prints I scored in a half-price sale at West Elm. Most important, however, I have a window. The view mostly consists of pigeons taking craps on the ledge, but it's mine, and unless I get promoted, I'll give it up over my cold, dead body.

Vik settles his dad—Mr. Ilin—in a chair and hands him the cup of coffee. Ilin Senior takes an enormous slurp of coffee and beams at me. "Awesome doughnuts."

"You're welcome." And he truly is.

"So." I sit down behind my desk. Texting is so much easier than this face-to-face stuff.

Vik flashes me a smile. "I really am here to sort out my old man's finances."

"I have it handled." Vik's dad sounds downright grumpy, so I don't think it's the first time they've had this conversation.

"Bullshit," Vik sums up. "You couldn't pay your rent because you'd stashed the cash underneath your couch. What wasn't there was tucked into coffee cans.

None of it was in the fucking bank where it belonged, so you wrote a check that bounced."

He has a point.

"Okay. Since you're a last-minute addition to my schedule, I haven't had a chance to review your port-folio yet, so let's see if I can get a sense of what your assets are."

The old guy pats his crotch. "Keep my assets right here."

Ooo-kay.

Vik clearly inherited his sense of humor from his dad.

CHAPTER ELEVEN

Vik

I MAKE HARPER NERVOUS. She fidgets with the folder she's holding and then twitches the sassy bow tie on the front of her blouse. Fuck me, but that blouse is killing me. The woman has a serious fetish for all things bow-tied and I'm torn between wondering how she'd feel if I showed up at her place wearing just a bow tie and nothing more, and asking her if she'd let me tie her up.

Or untie her.

One swift tug and that bow comes undone. It taunts me as she sashays across the room toward me, all long legs in that prim, black skirt. Am I hard? Fuck yeah, especially when she slides on a pair of glasses. Today's glasses are bright green, beer bottle green, grass green, fucking Emerald City green. A man can only hope she's got the panties to match.

"You got a different pair of glasses for each outfit?"

Harper opens her mouth, maybe to shoot me down, but my dad busts in first.

116

INKED

"So how long have you two known each other?"

Getting my dad here this morning took a combination of bribery and blackmail. Given his never-ending interest in my love life (which is nonexistent, unlike my sex life), I may have let him think that Harper's potential girlfriend material and that he'd be doing me a favor by giving me an excuse to visit her office. Given his unwavering interest in pairing me off, he was happy to help.

Harper looks at him over the edge of her glasses. "Is our being acquaintances a problem?"

"Not at all. You two make a cute couple. You want my blessing, you got it." My dad polishes off doughnut number two as he drops that conversational bomb, and I don't think the look of satisfaction on his face has anything to do with the maple glazed he just consumed. Nope. He's convinced that I've finally found me a girl—and he's not wrong. It's just that we're fuck buddies rather than lovers, and he's gonna find that disappointing.

Harper inhales sharply. Yeah, she's got something to say. "Your son and I are friends, Mr. Ilin."

It's cute how she pokers up. Unfortunately, her righteous indignation is wasted because with each agitated breath she takes, the buttons on her blouse gape. Her eyes sparkle with something. Ire, gas, sheer orneriness—I don't care. She's beautiful. Plus, there's no way I don't admire the show she's putting on for me. I lean sideways just a little. Can't quite tell if that's a beige bra or a white bra she's rocking.

"Eyes up here," she says drily.

See? I still blame her.

My dad nudges me. Any harder and he'd crack a rib. "Always listen to the lady you're dating."

Harper's gaze swings toward him, a look of complete *what the fuck* painted on her pretty face. She's not taking the news of our coupledom without some protests, it seems.

I stretch out my legs, my boots invading her space beneath the desk. She jumps like I've goosed her and glares at me. *Go along with it*, I mouth silently.

She jerks her attention back to the folder in front of her. "I'm not sure how we can help you."

I don't miss a beat. "I can make suggestions."

The look she levels on me is glacial. Christ, that just makes me want to warm her up. "Perhaps you should step outside while I discuss your father's finances with your father."

I shake my head. You know, just in case I'm no longer speaking English. "I stay."

She shoves her glasses farther up her nose and gets this cute, irritated look on her face. "Give me a reason."

Under normal circumstances, she wouldn't be wrong about asking me to leave. But these aren't normal circumstances. Sure, my old man mistakenly thinks that Harper and I are dating. He also routinely thinks it's 1955, that it's Monday and that he has a bank account full of dollars just begging to be spent. Oh, and he also hasn't filed a tax return in five years.

I lean forward, cross my arms over my chest. Harper's eyes fly to my chest and then shoot back to my face. Since we're at her work and we're not alone, I do my best to ignore her interest. I'll remind her about it later. What Harper really likes are numbers, so I'll give her that.

"Item one? He's my dad. That trumps everything as far as I'm concerned. We're family, so I've got him. Item two? He's been supplementing his social security by making personal loans to his neighbors in Happy Vegas Valley Trailer Park. And since he charges 27 percent interest, he hasn't done too badly."

"It's like them small incubator start-up thingies where you crowdfund crap," my old man says defensively. "It was practically public service, if you ask me."

"Item three," I continue, "he stores his profits in a fucking shoe box. For diversity's sake, he also has 'accounts' in his mattress, his bookcase and under his sofa as previously mentioned. That means he's got lots of cash, and no idea how to get it back on the books."

Harper visibly winces. I'm guessing that the shoe box organizational system is her idea of the seventh level of hell. She starts asking my dad a series of questions about how much income he's interested in seeing from his investments and how risk-averse he is.

I snort. My old man and risk are best friends.

For a few seconds, there's nothing but blissful quiet in Harper's office. My dad works on polishing off his muffin, and Harper works out my dad, shifting papers from one stack to another. Where I see a mess, she sees a goddamned puzzle—and she's about to fit the pieces together. And when my dad excuses himself "to find the little boy's room," I seize my chance.

I'm out of my seat and around her desk in two seconds flat. Yes, I'm crowding her. Yes, I have no intention of moving anywhere but closer.

"Space. Give me space." She swats my thigh without looking up.

Nope. That sure as fuck doesn't work for me.

I pull her up out of her seat, slide those glasses off her nose and kiss her. It's a quick kiss because I don't know how long my old man will be gone, but it definitely won't be long enough for the kind of sexual marathon I want when I look at Harper. Christ, she's gorgeous.

Since I have to work with the time I have, I swing her around, shove her folders to one side and plant her cute ass on the freshly cleared real estate. "Have you ever come on your desk?"

"What?" The look on her face is awesome—part cranky, part embarrassed...and part curious. Harper definitely has a dirty side.

"I'll take that as a no. Up." I tug on the hem of her skirt.

She lifts obediently before she thinks about it. "No, wait. What are you doing?"

"Showing you some friendly appreciation." I fold her skirt up to her waist because Harper won't be a fan of wrinkles. She likes her shit well-organized and pressed. She squirms, but I don't think she's trying to get away. More like I've got her off balance and she's deciding if she likes it.

Her panties are a barely-there scrap of yellow, the kind of thong that yields zero panty line. It's probably a purely practical decision on Harper's part, but I can see the outline of her pussy peeking through the lacy front like it's saying *hello*. Or *touch me*. I'm always happy to give a lady what she wants. I yank them off and shove her legs over my shoulder.

"You're gonna have to be quiet, Harper. Can you do that for me?"

She glares at me, but she doesn't close her legs. Of course, given the fact that my shoulders are now holding her thighs apart, shutting me out is gonna be difficult. But her face pinkens up and she's not saying *no*. Since we both know I'm always gonna listen to her, that's a big *hell, yeah* in my book. I get straight to work on making sure that Harper has a very, very good day at work.

She's already wet and slick, so somebody's been thinking naughty, work-inappropriate thoughts. I run my thumbs up her thighs and open her up wide. She squeak-moans, but she keeps the volume low enough that the rest of the office won't come rushing in. Good girls deserve rewards, so I kiss her.

I cover her clit with my mouth, circling it with my tongue.

She moans a little louder and promptly slaps her hand over her mouth. I forgot to specify staying still, so she starts wiggling and bucking around her desk as I tongue her. She tastes even better than I remember. I lick and suck, shoving two fingers deep inside her as I look for and find her G-spot. She moans my name and tenses.

Harper's not a screamer. We established that two weeks ago, when I fucked her senseless against the window in her hotel room. She just sort of melts, coming undone at the edges as she comes. She shudders and tenses and then makes all these cute whimpering noises as I kiss harder and deeper, making her ride my mouth until she's done.

She flops back on her desk, panting. She's all loose and relaxed, and she looks like she just had a mid-day orgasm. At work. When there are a million suit-wearing people walking past her closed door. She must remember that because about two seconds after I switch her brain off with the mother of all orgasms, she sits bolt upright. Guess the thinking part of her has come back online.

"Your father," she whispers, her face flaming red. She practically throws herself at me, trying to scramble off the desk. Since she's come and I've had my fun, I help her off if only because the way her legs wobble for a second makes me feel like a fucking king. "I'm at *work*."

"Think of me as a fringe benefit." I pull her skirt down and retie the bow at her throat. I always put away my toys when I'm done playing with them. Her panties, however, go in my pocket. Since I don't get to come, I deserve a souvenir for later.

"He thinks we're *dating*."

"Yeah." I scrub a hand over my forehead. Harper's scent is all over me and my dick's imitating an iron bar. "Got to admit that's a challenge, but here's what I'm thinking. We're friends, right?"

"Right." She stares at me, suspicion written all over her gorgeous face.

"So that means I have your back," I explain. "And you have mine. Right now, I need to keep my old man happy. What I really want is for him to get off my back about dating someone, so if he thinks we're a couple, problem solved."

"But we're not dating," she protests.

"No," I agree. "I'm not a relationship guy. I don't want to be your boyfriend—just your fuck buddy."

"And friends," she says.

"Friends who bang," I agree. I can hear my old man coming down the hall. He's loud, but he sounds happy and he's taking his sweet time. I suspect this is intentional—after all, we're family and he knows exactly what *he'd* be doing if the situation were reversed and he had a hot investment banker alone in an office.

"He's an old man and he's confused. He'll likely forget the meeting ten minutes after he leaves, so no worries. All you have to do is pretend for now. You do that for me, and I'll owe you one."

From the way Harper's eyes widen, she thinks *owe you one* is code for doing her right in the bedroom. She doesn't say no, though. She stays silent until my dad wanders back in and we resume our meeting.

Exactly thirty minutes after we barged through her office door, she's steering us back out. For two seconds I contemplate refusing to go, but that won't get me anywhere. Plus, my dad really does need her help—and Harper will rock what she does. She'd never settle for coming in second or third when she could be the winner.

"I'll do my best, Mr. Ilin." She pats my dad on the hand and he beams back at her, completely smitten.

I put my old man into the elevator and then I pause, running my fingers down her cheek. Nobody can see us here, not unless they pull the security tapes, so it's safe enough. She's earned the same respect I have when I'm on club business—I won't jeopardize her job.

"Think about my offer," I say. "Booty call. You. Me. Maybe a real fucking bed an entire night this time."

"I—"

She shakes her head like she's got no idea what to say to me. *Yes* works just fine.

"Bring the shoes." I step inside the elevator and let the door slide closed.

CHAPTER TWELVE

Harper

MEN THINK ABOUT sex a lot. Researchers have spent thousands of man-hours studying the issue, and it's a hard one, all puns intended. And so while it might be a stereotype that men think about sex 24/7, they definitely do it often.

And so do women.

Especially *this* woman.

Turns out I'm an overachiever in the thinking-about-sex department, particularly when it comes to Vik. Professionalism flies out the window, and when I work on his dad's portfolio, I daydream about having sex with him. Vik that is—not his dad. Freud would have a field day with that one. My week goes something like this: research investments for Mr. Ilin Senior, contemplate sweeping Vik away to Bora Bora, Paris or the top-floor penthouse at the Bellagio, and telling him he has no choice but to indulge in all my dirty fantasies because I've just earned his dad a million bucks. Drag my head back to the numbers on the computer screen in front of me. Rinse and repeat.

Don't judge. It's no more twisted (or likely) than all those billionaires-buying-virgins schemes that top the bestseller lists.

In reality, I put together a kick-ass portfolio for his dad, and then I do the same thing for ten other new clients. Yes, I've been a busy girl. So busy that on Friday, one of the senior partners stops by to congratulate me and let me know that *they've* got their eyes on me. I can practically smell the promotion.

Better yet, I outperform all my colleagues, which means that I win the Friday prize, a bottle of Veuve Clicquot. Senior management sees the prize-giving as a chance to foster a little friendly competition between us junior firm members, while doling out cheap pats on the back for another successful sixty-hour work week. The champagne's a fun bonus, but it's not the real prize and everyone knows it. There are five of us junior planners, and we're cheerfully cutthroat about the business of getting ahead. No one's going to kneecap me in a parking structure or poach my idea, but everyone wants to be The One, the junior employee who gets the golden invitation to join the big boys and girl at the next level. In this spirit, my coworkers hand me a package of straws to go with my new bottle of fizz, so that I can *better suck up.* I laugh so hard I almost pee myself.

I may not have scored me a badass biker, but my Friday drunky is now a sure thing. I grab my bottle and my things and head home. *Home.* My new condo

still feels unfamiliar and sterile, like I'm camped out
in a super-chic office or Airbnb. Instead of tackling
the sadly small mountain of moving boxes (honestly
it's more hill than mountain), I fill up my kitchen sink
with ice cubes and submerge my champagne. I'm light
on glasses thanks to the Douche's self-serving divi-
sion of our household goods, so after I change into
my pajamas, I end up drinking out of a juice glass
decorated with red cherries. I'm not entirely certain
that's a regulation-size pour, but down the hatch it
goes. In the spirit of adulting, I drop a few raspberries in there, thus covering one if not two of the major
food groups.

The three glasses of champagne I down in the next
hour undoubtedly explain how my thumbs end up
searching for Vik's contact info in my phone. I plan
out my approach while I finish glass number four. The
beauty of drinking and planning is that every idea
seems like genius. Instead of a carefully weighted
list of pros and cons, my thoughts gravitate more toward *why the fuck not?*

Remember how I said that women think about
doing it, too? I'm all about sexual equality. In fact, the
number of times I've fantasized about Vik this week
puts me firmly in overachiever territory. Banging,
knocking uglies, shaboinking… I've thought about
it and then mentally mapped out the steps it would
take to bring those activities to fruition.

Okay, fine. Maybe I do spend too much time making lists and outlining steps, but if I ever get my hands

on Vik Ilin, I'll be making both of us happy. My
phone buzzes in my hand.

Huh.

Some hussy has propositioned my biker while I've
been thinking deep thoughts. I have no idea how this
happened, but she's quite blunt and straightforward.

ME: U busy? If not, come have sex with me. Plz.

She has lovely manners.

She's also pretty shameless for someone drunk-
texting at 11:50 p.m.

Under ordinary, less inebriated circumstances,
I'd give that girl a standing ovation. Self-control's
not her strong point, but she's identified a want and
gone for it.

Fuck me.

What was I thinking? I've just texted Vik and tried
to set up a booty call. You know how some corporate
email programs have that nifty feature where you can
recall an email after you send it because instead of
attaching the business proposal your boss requested,
you forwarded last night's home porn movie? I totally
need that now for my texts. Sure, I pretended to be
adding spontaneity to my life. But now that the universe is all *wish granted*?

I need a do-over.

A delete key.

An enormous freaking Magic Eraser to blot the
last two minutes out of my life and Vik's memory.

11:53.

11:54.

It's like watching the countdown clock on a deto-
nator that's wired up to a ton of TNT. Any second
now, Vik will glance down at his phone and see I've
propositioned him. Courage seems like a great idea,
the ultimate personal high, an absolute must-do on my
personal bucket list. Now that I've taken the plunge,
however, I realize that the problem with personal
highs is the *plunge*. I'm free-falling off a fucking
emotional mountain and the ground's coming up fast.

11:56.

11:57.

I'm not good at waiting. Timetables are my friend.
Perhaps Vik is asleep. Or his phone is dead. Or he's
busy banging some other chick. No, scratch that. Perhaps he dropped his phone in the toilet and it's permanently ruined and he'll never, ever see my text
message.

Asking him to come over.

For sex.

I pour another glass of champagne (number five
for those of you keeping track at home). Of course,
he could simply be uninterested. We've had sex, but
maybe he's the kind of man who doesn't vacation at
the same property twice, no matter how fabulous the
first experience. Just because I'm up for round two
doesn't mean that he is.

12:07.

Sometimes you need to change your plans.

I fire up my laptop and get ready to go with Plan B:
retail therapy. I swing by Amazon, from whence all

good things come, and fill up my cart with a brand-new, designer wardrobe for a fantasy trip to the Maldives that will stifle the lingering humiliation caused by Vik's silence. Tomorrow, I'll empty the cart and replace its contents with the far more practical cat food and toilet paper deliveries that I actually need, but for tonight...I *totally* need a three-hundred-dollar silk sundress for my hypothetical three-thousand-dollar-a-night bungalow. For that kind of price, Amazon had better be including Chris Hemsworth or Pierce Brosnan in the box.

CHAPTER THIRTEEN

Vik

Tonight I went to church.

Don't look so shocked. It's a Hard Riders thing, a weekly MC meeting that every brother is expected to attend. Missing one meeting nets you a fine. The second time you ditch earns a personal, hands-on explanation of the attendance policy. Third time? You don't want to go there.

We're not big on rules, although respect is king. This means I've had my phone off for most of the night. We need to up our security, and doing so requires planning. Too many brothers have been shot at or taken hostage this year. Last time it happened, we got our brother back, but several of the Black Dogs MC had gone up on charges for the kidnapping, and it looked like shit might stick. Rev's old lady was making noises about it, too, because her brother, Rocker, was one of those who took a ride downtown in the back of a cop car. Stupid fuck had run drugs and guns. He's looking at some serious time.

The kidnapped brother didn't come out of it the same, either. He's making noises about reaching out to the other club now that they've had their come-to-Jesus moment with the law. Rest of us aren't convinced that the Black Dogs MC have given up on drug-dealing and the cartels. He keeps hinting he has leverage with the other club now that he's been up close and personal with them, but other Hard Riders suggested the *up close and personal* actually occurred with a Black Dogs hanger-on. Specifically, a hanger-on with a super-awesome, miracle pussy. That accusation led to a fight tonight and the argument still isn't settled.

Sucked to be my brother, though, if he's jonesing for a girl who belongs to a rival club. Some shit's just too Romeo and Juliet for words, and I'm not the only brother to notice because Prez has taken to calling him Romeo. I threatened to tattoo his new name on his ass.

Automatically, I turn my phone on as I head out to the parking lot and discover Santa Claus has come early.

HARPER: U busy? If not, come have sex with me. Plz.

Why I'm so tied up in knots about this girl, I don't know. Maybe it's listening to my dad ask if I've met someone. Or maybe it's because inking and fucking go hand in hand more than you'd think. Harper isn't the first to climb into my chair and then drop her panties. She's had a rough time with her ex, and she deserves some sweet in her life. Part of me still thinks hunting the guy down and teaching him some manners is the best idea I've had in a long time. The rest of me thinks we should just focus on getting Harper naked and wet. Get our priorities right.

Romeo shoulders me hard. "Are you buuuuussy, Vik? Or you gonna put out for her?"

"Fuck off." I keep walking toward my bike. Yes, of course I'm headed over to Harper's place. I like her, I like sex, so that's a win-win situation right there.

Romeo's apparently not done giving me shit, however, because he snatches my phone out of my hand. He has to be the biggest brother in the club, and he fills in whenever we need a bouncer or someone requires an ass-kicking. Still not sure how the Black Dogs got the jump on him. We wrestle briefly because I'm determined to get my phone back. I fucking end up on the bottom, too, because the brother's built like a linebacker.

"You gonna hang here?" Romeo laughs down at me. "Or you got other plans?"

He grins at me and reaches between us to shove my phone back into my pocket.

"My dick's got other plans for tonight," I grumble, holding back my own smile. "Don't get too close."

"So you're headed over to see the lovely Harper?" He rolls off me.

"Yeah." I sit up, checking to make sure everything still works. Harper won't enjoy me quite so much if I'm bruised. She likes looking at me.

Romeo slaps me on the back and reaches down a hand. "Who is she?"

I let him pull me up. "None of your business."

Not that she should be my business, either, but we've already established that I don't always do the right thing. Which has to be why I race to Harper's place. Lucky I don't get picked up for breaking every traffic law. She's got a new rental in one of those swank, super-modern high-rise buildings, the kind of place where the windows don't open because the people inside are living in an air-conditioned bubble. Not sure I see the appeal myself, but it's not my call.

I'm standing in front of Harper's door before I realize I probably should have called first. Or texted. Fucking sent a carrier pigeon with roses. Doesn't matter now because I'm here.

I knock. Then fucking knock again. And again. I'm about ready to text Romeo to get his ass over here and help me bust the thing down when she finally yanks the door open.

"Vik?" She sounds part horrified, part dazed.

What the fuck?

"You texted me."

She's wearing a pair of silky pajamas covered with a ridiculous quantity of pink and orange butterflies. The top is one of those camisoles that button up the front and the fabric's sheer enough that I can see the outline of her bra and the soft curve of her belly. Best wrapping paper ever for my Christmas present.

She crosses her arms over her chest. "An hour and a half ago."

"Didn't see an expiration date on your text, so unless you want to fuck in your hallway, let's go inside."

Her mouth falls open and I smell champagne and raspberries. "Excuse me?"

"I'm just keeping my word." Christ, I'm practically a Boy Scout. "I offered to be your booty call. You called, so here I am."

While she splutters, I lean down and kiss her. Our kiss is way too quick but gives me enough time to discover that she tastes like champagne, raspberries and Harper. Not sure what that is other than pure fucking heaven. Letting go requires more self-control than I'd like to admit, but I have plans and it's time to put them into action. Step one? I shrug off my club vest and then whip my T-shirt over my head. I do my best work naked, and something tells me that stripping down in a public place is guaranteed to get a response out of Harper.

Three, two, one...

Sure enough, she goes ballistic.

"You can't do that here!" She grabs whatever she can, yanking at me. Not sure what her objective is, but since it involves her hands touching me in about a hundred different, bare places, I approve. Fuck, she's fun. I start working on my belt.

"Inside," she hisses, hooking her fingers in my belt. Since my dick's huge and my pants hang low, she skims my goodies and jolts backward. I'm commando beneath the denim. While I try not to spontaneously combust, she reaches around me to grab my shirt and vest from the floor outside her door. Guess I'm gonna be her not-so-little dirty secret.

In it is.

"You," she snaps as soon as I'm safely out of the hallway and the door's closed. "You're impossible."

She slaps my chest with her hand, then stares down at her fingers lying right there over my heart. She looks surprised. Not sure if it's my ink or my muscles that's got her going. I'd play show-and-tell with her, but I don't need her distracted right now. Plus, I'm semihard already, so I have better plans for our time together.

I tug her into my arms and spin her around until her back's against the wall. "I'm fucking easy for you."

Probably should have brought wine or flowers or at least asked for a tour of her new place, but we've both waited long enough. Then I'm lifting her up, spreading her legs around my hips and pinning her against the wall. Only thing between my dick and her pussy are my jeans and her shorts, and that's not gonna keep me out of heaven.

She makes the cutest little growling sound in her throat, so I'm half expecting her to go for my balls with her right knee when she surprises me by going to work on my belt buckle. The leather slaps against my abs as she pulls it free so fast I almost get rug burn.

"Don't mark the merchandise." I nip her ear. "You spank my dick with that shit, and I'll get even."

She makes a scoffing sound, even as I wrap the belt around her wrists—loosely because I'm not *that*

much of a jerk—and pull her hands above her head.
I give her a moment to realize her predicament, and
then I lean down and kiss her.

She tastes even better than I remember, and that's
before she shoves her tongue deep into my mouth.
Not sure she knows I'm the one who's in charge here,
and somehow that just sets me on fire more. Fucking need this woman bad because until I'm inside
her, filling up that place she's got for me between her
legs, I'm nowhere.

So I kiss her back, going harder, deeper, until we're
pushing and fighting each other with our mouths because neither of us will back down. Our mouths clash,
all teeth and tongues, and it's wet and slippery, and
absolutely fucking perfect. We don't kiss pretty but
somehow we fit together. We're burning together, and
I don't need words to know that. When I pull back, I'm
panting, and so is she. We're belting out the same chorus of the same song, and it's all halle-fucking-lujah.
I'm not alone in what I'm feeling here.

"Tell me yes," I say. "Also? You got some fucking
specific requests, you make them now."

"Or what?" Her words come out in a pant, and
her tits are heaving up and down like we've just run
a marathon.

"Or you won't get a turn." I nip her unmarked
ear so that now she's got a matched set and drag my
thumb over her cheek. "And you won't like that half
as much as I will."

She glares at me but then she raises her hands over

her head and links them behind my neck. The leather of my belt rubs against me, holding us close.

"You suck," she announces.

"Duly noted." I can't help laughing. "But I do other things, as well."

She shoves at my shoulder, but I don't budge. I'm bigger than her, plus the way she's wriggling against me, I don't think she really wants me to go anywhere. Except down. She smells amazing, like cookies or vanilla, and her body's all sweet curves just begging for a good licking.

She bites my lower lip, and now I'm the one growling. "What was that for?"

"You made me wait. Don't do that again," she orders, looking completely unrepentant.

I shouldn't be this turned on. She bit me, for fuck's sake. Her pretty mouth forms a perfect O that just begs for my dick. My entire body jumps to attention, ready to make that fantasy come true.

"Say it. And don't fucking bite me again, or I'll bite back."

"Yes," she growls.

I twist a hand in her hair, pulling her head back until I have an all-access pass to her mouth. "You like this?"

Her mouth firms, but I'm not giving her a chance to fuck with me. I pull just a little harder and then I kiss her hard and fast, shoving my tongue between her sassy, stubborn lips. And she gives back as good as she gets, shoving against me and driving her own tongue into my mouth. She won't let me dominate her, and I kind of don't want to. I like this. I like the way she more than meets me halfway and won't take my shit.

So I kiss her while she kisses me, her nails scratching my bare back. Bet she's drawing blood. Bet she's inking me in her own way. I fucking love that I'll wear her mark tomorrow on my skin, but she's wearing too many clothes. I pop the buttons open on her top, yank down the cotton bra hiding her tits from me and get my hands on her nipples. I should probably take the time to appreciate her underwear but right now it's just in the way of my worshipping her right.

Because I'm gonna take care of her properly. Make her see the stars, a whole fucking galaxy of sexual pleasure—or just me. Sure, I'm getting inside her, but it won't be without benefits for her. Her breasts pop right out into my hands, the nipples tightening as I rub my thumbs over them. She arches into me, moaning another demand. Fucking love that she knows what she wants.

Me.

And I'm all hers.

Except she's not done talking or thinking, which is something I really need to work on because if I'm doing my job right, rational thought should have been discarded along with her bra. "Lock the door?"

"That a request or a question?" I squeeze her nipples, working them between my fingers.

"Do it," she moans.

Fuck if I'm letting her go, so I walk us over to the door, my hands cupping her ass, and flip the lock.

"We good now?"

When she nods, I set her down, her back against the door. I'm betting she won't be happy if I tear her cute little PJs off her, so it's time to strip. I shove her shirt down her arms, follow it up with the straps of her bra and then go to work on her shorts. I take a brief second to appreciate the hot-pink thong with a big-ass bow parked right over her clit. FYI? That's the best kind of X-marks-the-spot.

I yank my jeans open. Finding a bed seems like a waste of time when I could be balls-deep in Harper. Dick free enough, I grab a condom out of my wallet. It's not my classiest move but Harper likes feeling safe and I'd never do anything to hurt her. Her eyes get wider as I roll the rubber on. Taking her bareback would be something, but that's not for tonight.

She watches me as I suit up, her eyes following my hands as they stroke that shit into place and give my dick a warm-up twist, kind of like a competitive diver throwing in a bonus reverse tuck and a couple dozen somersaults because the judges are watching and that high score beckons. I don't need Harper to tell me that she doesn't do this kind of wild, crazy shit. She's as buttoned-up and cute as the pajamas lying on the floor, but buttons were made to be undone and Harper's fucking perfect. I love that she flies apart for me—now I just need her to do it with me. And like she's reading my mind, she leans up and takes my mouth with hers, kissing me for all she's worth.

So much for foreplay.

I open up, lifting her up. Her hands grab my shoulders, her legs going around my waist. You see that fit? We're absolutely perfect together, and I forget all about being her booty call or her one-time-and-never-again man. She won't forget this when we're over. I won't let her. I'm starting to realize I want something more from her, even if I don't know what that *more* is.

Not yet.

I raise her up and set her on my cock. Just the tip of me teasing that hot, wet doorway to heaven.

Goddamn she's something else.

Hottest thing ever, the way she moans and tries to take me. Right now? She'd let me do whatever I want with her. She's trusting me to make her come hard, and she's not wrong. I push into her, finding her clit with my thumb as she takes me deep. My balls tighten and holding on becomes a fucking torture mission. I work her clit in small, hard circles, and she bucks. Desperate for more. I slam home.

Harper's my kind of girl. She sucks in a breath—releases it on a moan that makes me wish we could go all night because goddamn she likes this. Her hips roll as she rides me, my hands helping her to find the rhythm that's gonna send us both over the edge. I can smell the sweet, salty scent of her and me together and I jerk my fingers away from her clit, licking them. Got to have my taste, and sure enough, she's sweeter than all the fucking cupcakes in this world.

I grab onto her ass, working her on my dick, and she exhales long and soft. And then there's nothing but heat licking through me as I drive into her, the whole world narrowing down to this one amazing woman. I want to make it last forever, but my dick's about to blow. I pound her hard, and she's slamming down to meet me, her nails biting into my shoulders.

She squeezes.

Holds me tight.

It's fucking game over for me and I shoot into her as she comes hard, jerking and twisting. Then she throws her arms around my neck, burying her face against my throat as she loses it. Her pussy clamps down, and I feel each squeeze and pulse as she comes hard. Never felt better.

Can't imagine what I do now.

I've had my share of women, but Harper's someone special, and not just because she's got a magic pussy that makes me come so hard that I'm the one seeing stars. Stars, the sun, the moon and an entire nebulae of shit I never imagined or deserved. Harper might be uptight, buttoned-up and way too *grown* up, but she's also a revelation. No way will I pull out and walk away now.

CHAPTER FOURTEEN

Harper

AFTER VIK BANGS me senseless against my own door, he decides it's time to christen every room in my new place. When I point out the ambitious scope of this plan, he suggests a compromise. He makes me come in each room, and then we end up in my bed. He steals a selfie of the two of us together (from the neck up) to send to his dad, who's still on Vik's case to date "someone nice."

Vik says I'm perfect for the job.

I'm not getting out of bed for at least a day. Too bad there's no Fitbit for sex—I'd have burned a million calories by now. Vik grins down at me. Having me sprawled beneath him appears to be his favorite position, although he doesn't discriminate. We've done it up against the wall, on the floor and doggy style. Right now I've got the best view ever of his gorgeous face. His eyes crinkle up at the corners because the man's that goddamned happy. Or possibly I'm blurry-eyed from all the sex.

"Let's do this again," he says.

Something throbs between my legs, either in anticipation or a warning shot that any more sex and I might be permanently broken.

"Can you die from too much coming?"

He drops a kiss on top of my head. "Not sure we should put that to the test. Sore?"

"A little." I roll over, burying my face in the pillow.

"You want me to kiss it better?"

"I'll take a rain check." There's no way I can hold back my yawn—the man has worn me out.

Vik freezes and there's this moment of awkward silence. Clearly, I've read more into tonight than I should have. Maybe I shouldn't have mentioned the possibility of a next time, but I was mostly joking. I know I shouldn't push for anything more, and frankly I don't know what I want.

Other than his dick.

Vik's dick is my favorite.

And I think I have some body parts that he's rather fond of, too.

"Not sure what's happening here, but I gotta tell you something," he says finally.

"Okay?" I'm really not in the mood for the letdown speech. Last time he snuck out, leaving a cute note. I'd like a little more than that, but I'm honestly not sure how much more.

"You keep calling me, and I'll be the best booty call ever. I promise you this, sweetheart. I'll be your best. Got an orgasm gift-wrapped, with your name on it. Helps to have a face to show my old man, too—

makes him happy to think I'm seeing someone nice. You want to do this again?"

"We can," I say slowly. "And I have to admit that I want to, but I've got to be honest. I'm in the market for a long-term, forever relationship, and that's not us."

He shrugs easily. "Yeah, I'm not into anything permanent, either, babe. Like I said, booty call. You call me when you need some, and I'll call you. It doesn't have to be complicated."

"So just until I meet Mr. Right?" Okay, so I sound less doubtful than I should when he proposes no-strings-attached sex. But his dick's amazing, and I like the guy. We could have fun together.

"That works," he says easily. "I'll even throw in a freebie and help you screen potential dates."

I snort. "You're going to play matchmaker to my Yentl?"

He rubs a palm up and down my back. My tattoo's healed and there's not a lick of pain now. "I'm not gonna get in your way, Harper. We'll do what you want on your terms. You meet a nice guy, good for you. You meet someone not so great, I'll be your own personal bouncer."

It's the craziest idea I've ever heard. But I like Vik, I like his penis, and it's not like I'll stroll out onto the Strip this afternoon and stumble over the perfect man. So why not enjoy Vik in the meantime? We're good together, and I think we could be friends. Plus, there's the whole incredible orgasms thing. The man's a total giver in that department, and it would be a shame to not take advantage.

"Okay." I'm weak. Completely, utterly weak. I blame that on the hot sex. "I'll call you. You'll call me. Somehow this will all work out."

He drops a kiss onto my forehead. "I'll be the best booty call ever. Just wait and see."

Yeah. There's no doubt in my mind that the man can deliver. I drift off to sleep, probably wearing a big, goofy smile because the man has fucked all the common sense straight out of my head. I've never felt this giddy about a hookup. That's never happened before. I mean, he's also my first attempt at casual sex, but I'm giving myself an A for effort. Letting him go would be disappointing.

When I wake up minutes, hours, who-knows-how-much later, there's a heavy, muscled arm draped over my stomach. I consider sucking in my belly because there's more curve there than I like, but on the other hand, Vik doesn't seem to mind. So I give up on miraculously transforming into a Victoria's Secret model and trace my fingers over the ink on his forearm. He has matching bands, dark geometrical scrolls of mandalas that circle upward from the tops of his hands. But because some things can't wait, no matter how beautiful he is, I shift his arm and make for the edge of the bed.

He grunts and rolls over. "You up? You need me to go?"

"Call of nature," I overshare. He nods, settling back into the bed. God, he's gorgeous. Because I've had my fingers in it for the better part of the night, his blond hair is tousled so he looks like some kind of sleeping bear. It cascades over his bare shoulders, almost reaching his chest. He snags my pillow, though, so it's not like he's a saint.

After pulling on his T-shirt to cover up my ass, I grab my phone and snap a picture. Some things are even better with photographic proof. I take care of my business in the bathroom and then step out onto my teeny-tiny balcony. If I twist my head and lean dangerously sideways, I actually have a view of the Strip. While I admire the sliver of pyramid that I can see, I call Brooklyn. That girl's got a sick penchant for running at the crack of dawn, so I'm betting she's already up. Sure enough, she answers.

When she picks up, I just blurt it out. "I had sex."

"Congratulations." She sounds faintly out of breath, so I'm betting she's getting her jog on. "Anybody I know?"

In answer, I send her the picture I took of Vik.

"You screwed the tattoo artist?"

"He's a biker, too, and he's freaking gorgeous," I point out. Strictly in the spirit of being honest, of course, and not because I feel like screaming or doing handstands because I, Harper George, have just banged the ever-living daylights out of a man who is very clearly a ten-plus on the hotness scale.

"Are you seeing each other?" Brooklyn's breathing escalates, so either she's just as affected by Vik's picture as I am, or she's definitely running.

"He's my booty call." God, that sounds weird. I mean, it also sounds downright fantastic, but this isn't something I have any experience with.

I can practically hear Brooklyn rolling her eyes. "You've had your hands on that man and once was enough?"

"We have an arrangement." I hope she doesn't fall over laughing. "We're going to call each other whenever we want sex."

"Wow." For a moment, she says nothing.

"Brooklyn?"

"I'm trying to imagine this," she says. "Which is fun but I'm also a little worried about you."

"Did you look at that picture? We should be cracking champagne to celebrate," I protest.

"Booty calls can be dangerous." She sighs. "It's like buying the ten-dollar box of Star Wars Legos with the super-cool Darth Vader and then suddenly you're upgrading to the four-million-piece Death Star set and every time you step barefoot on the carpet, you find another super-pointy, overlooked piece."

"Is Vik Darth Vader or the Death Star in this example?"

"He's trouble. Hot, gorgeous, bad-boy trouble. He's going to look prettier and easier until you take him out of his box to play, and you need to be careful you don't get hurt."

She's just looking out for me, I remind myself. "Duly noted."

"Okay." She sighs again, sounding a little happier. "But you still have to tell me all the details when we get together, okay? And you're buying since you're the one with the naked hottie in her bed."

We say goodbye and I tiptoe back inside. Or try to.

A big, hard arm swings me around and off my feet. "Morning, babe."

Turns out my biker is even better than that first cup of morning coffee. We end up back in bed so he can kiss all my sore spots better, and then he takes off to do biker things, roaring off on his Harley before I have to invent awkward excuses to get him to leave.

CHAPTER FIFTEEN

Harper

"WHAT ABOUT THIS GUY?" I point to a dark-haired man on my phone while we wait for the light to change. Phone Guy is wearing a well-cut suit, a blue dress shirt open at the throat and no tie. The photo's classy but relaxed, so I think he should go in my keeper pile.

Vik turns his head so he can peer at Bachelor Number Twenty-Two. Since I'm wrapped around his back and straddling his bike, he's got limited viewing options. I wriggle, trying to get comfortable. While he makes a very sexy pillow, the man is *hard* and not just in the dick department. We've been hooking up for the last month, and the sex has been amazing. Vik may not be my forever man, but he's definitely turning out to be perfect for right now.

Taking the phone from my hands, he makes a non-committal noise. "You like the looks of him?"

It's surprisingly difficult to explain why some men look okay when others look all wrong. So far, no one has ticked all the boxes on the Fuck Him and Marry

Him list, but I have time. And while I look, I get hot sex on the side. As long as Vik wants to be friends with benefits, I'm up for it. So far, the orgasms have been as mind-blowing as I expected and the awkwardness has been far less.

"He chose a suit," I point out. "But no tie. He's got a great job and he's open to settling down with the girl of his dreams."

"He likes outdoor sports." Vik lazily hands the phone back to me. "And his idea of the best-ever date is canyoneering in Red Rock Canyon. Are you up for a two-hundred-foot rappel? Maybe you should practice, babe."

I'm sure Vik means that I should practice my outdoor skills, but right now I have other things on my mind. Big, sexy, bad-boy biker kinds of things. I blame Vik. He's the one who came by my place and suggested we go for a ride. He followed up his suggestion by prowling straight into my closet to rifle through my things in search of "riding gear." I got a little of my own back by "helping out" with his plan to dress me like his own personal Barbie doll by stripping down to my panties. That led to a very nice detour on the bed, but now we're riding. Or stopping for every red light in Vegas, which is also okay because I'm not in a hurry to get anywhere. I shove my phone back into my pocket as the light finally changes and we take off.

Vik on his bike gets my panties wet and the bike is just an added bonus. I love riding. It makes me feel like I'm hurtling down the world's shortest, fastest runway and that any second now I'll achieve liftoff and fly. My feet have yet to leave the ground when I'm with Vik, but I have high hopes. He takes me up the Strip today, and even in the sunlight, it's a fun riot of color. It's also extremely congested, which gives me plenty of time to check out the various attractions. The fountains explode as we ride past the Bellagio and I laugh. Seems like the kind of thing Vik would have planned. The man loves over-the-top gestures. Maybe he plans on ending our night by riding off into the sunset.

"Four o'clock," he says when we idle yet again at the next red light. I look and spot a group of men in business attire. "Red tie, navy blue suit, closest to the curb."

I let my gaze roam over Blue Suit as my arms tighten around Vik's waist, my chin resting on his shoulder. Vik's wearing his leather jacket, and beneath that, his club vest and a black T-shirt. His hair's pulled back into a ponytail, exposing the ink that edges his throat. More ink peeks out from beneath his jacket and on his knuckles. This is one of those perfect moments that I'd like to bottle up or freeze so that I can take it out and remember it over and over again in a month, a year, a lifetime. Eventually, Vik and I will part ways, and then these memories will be all I have left of him.

He's so beautiful.

I concentrate on breathing in and out as I tighten my hands over his stomach. He's so solid, so very, very present. Maybe it's because he's built like his

medieval namesake, but every inch of me is aware
of where I'm pressed up against him.

"Why him?"

"That suit didn't come cheap." Vik shrugs. "And
you see the way he pays attention to what his boys are
saying? He'll pay attention to you like that."

Blue Suit crosses in front of us, ushering the older
man in the group first. He's good-looking but not self-
absorbed. Vik's not wrong about his attractiveness,
but it's not like I could act on the recommendation.
What am I going to do, pass out a business card like
those guys who line the Vegas sidewalks handing out
cards for lap dances and private parties?

"Two o'clock," Vik says.

"I only need one man," I protest, even as I look.

"You didn't want the first guy," he growls.

No. No, I didn't.

Fortunately, once we leave the Strip behind us, we
pick up speed and Vik stops offering to hook me up.
He's decided to take me to Red Rock. And since he
promises I'll like it, I'm all in. After all, what's not to
like about the desert, some cliffs and tons of wildlife?

We abandon the bike in the parking lot, although
Vik grabs his saddlebags, slinging them over his
shoulder. Then he threads his fingers through mine
and heads past the obvious campsites. It's hot, the few
tents and RVs almost visibly steaming in the afternoon sunlight. A few steps into our walk, he passes
me a bottle of water. I'm not entirely certain if the
benefits of hydrating outweigh the dubious charms

of the campsite toilets. I much prefer doing my business in the Bellagio's marble stalls to squatting behind a manzanita bush.

Trust and promises of pleasure only go so far with this girl, however. The longer we walk, the more I want specifics. "Tell me exactly where we're going?"

The corners of his mouth quirk up. "You don't like surprises?"

He knows I don't. He teased me mercilessly when he spotted my paper planner. It's the deluxe Happy Planner model, and even though we're months from the end of the year, it weighs about ten pounds thanks to my liberal use of washi tape because I believe you can be both organized and pretty. Thank God he didn't spot my dream board when he rifled through my closet earlier today. I'd never hear the end of that.

"One mile." His fingers squeeze mine. That's the thing about Vik—he teases, but he also makes sure I always get what I need. He seems okay with my quirks. I take a moment to pause and set my Fitbit. This is going to be the mother lode of steps.

Vik's mile turns out to be more of an amble than a hike, if I'm honest. He takes me down a dirt trail, our hands still linked, and I split my time between staring at his butt and the scenery. The famous walls of Red Rock Canyon soar overhead, all stark rock and handfuls of scrubby bushes and grasses. I'm just starting to get into it when Vik stops, looks around and then steps. Off. The. Path.

Hello.

I've seen those movies, read those books.

You don't leave the path. EVER.

I dig in, planting my feet on the well-traveled path. Vik, of course, just grins at me. That smile of his... I'm in so much trouble.

"Problem, babe?"

I point to the trail (such as it is—it's not like he's taking me down a well-paved highway with sanctioned rest stops). "This is where we want to be, *honey buns.*"

Every time he calls by one of his ridiculous nicknames, I'm trying on a new one for him. I Googled an entire list and have them stored on my phone.

He tugs lightly on my hand. "Trust me."

And tugs again.

Somehow, just like that, I'm following him off the path and into the brush. After our closet encounter earlier today, I'm ready to jump him again. But we have to establish some boundaries, and I do need to get on with my life. I can't keep letting him do whatever he wants.

But as always, Vik squashes all my logical objections simply by tucking me into his side. He blazes a new path, holding the thornier branches aside for me, and making sure I'm good. If I have to have an up-close-and-personal encounter with Mother Nature, this isn't a bad way to do it. Vik smells fantastic, too, all leather and man instead of the usual Burberry Eau de Toilette I breathe in at work. He hums a heavy metal tune. Since the last time he came over hum-

ming he left me with a Metallica earworm, I'm prepared today. I review my Disney princess knowledge
and get my Pocahontas on. Bet my rendition of "Just
Around the Riverbend" can drown out his rock tunes.

He shoots me a sidelong glance and hums louder.
I counter, and before long we're both shout-singing at
the top of our lungs. God, he's the best kind of jack-
ass. If there's any nature around here, it's completely
drowned out by our noise. Ryan Seacrest will not be
begging us to join *American Idol* anytime soon.

"Time to stop." Vik slaps a big hand over my
mouth and I nip lightly at his fingers. Gag me, will
he? I'm about to up the ante and bite something else
when I hear the water.

I push his hand away. "Are we swimming?"

He swats my butt. "You bet."

The swimming hole comes into view, the blue-
green water so clear that I can see the rocks on the
bottom. Vik drops the bags by the side of the creek
and shucks his jacket and vest, hanging them on a
branch. Then he hauls his T-shirt over his head. Pleasure explodes through me. I love watching him, the
way he moves so confidently, attacking life head-
on. And even though I should question the stripping-
down-in-public thing, I don't. I just stand and stare.

He laughs, the sound low and rough. "Get naked,
Harper. I've been waiting to see you all day."

He makes it sound simple, as if we're not outside
where anyone could see us. This section of the river
may be private, but there can't possibly be any truly

secret swimming holes near Vegas. It's too hot, the weather too perfect for a dip, for those secrets to be kept for long. And yet I start to undress, sliding off the cute, wine-colored leather jacket I impulse-bought online after our first ride together. I toe off my boots, peeling my socks off even more quickly because stripteases are for satin and silk, not moisture-wicking cotton. Vik's shed his own boots, and his hands work his belt open.

"Let me," I whisper, and his fingers still on the buckle.

"Babe?"

I don't want to be *babe* or *sweetheart* or any of the half a dozen other pet names he probably uses on the women who come and go in his life. I want him to see *me*, to need me the way I'm starting to need him. I drop to my knees in front of him and finish what he's started.

The buckle gives beneath my fingers, and then I'm unbuttoning his jeans, forcing myself to move slowly, to wait for his heated curse, even though I want to take him now, to swallow him whole and hang on to him, adding more perfect moments to my secret collection. I cup his balls through the denim. The hot, heavy weight fills my palm, a hard promise of what this man can do for me.

"Please," I whisper.

Vik's hands tangle in my ponytail, tilting my head back. He's fighting for control, but I want him all the way undone, and instinctively I know this is the way to do it. Just as soon as I undo the buttons, he'll be all mine.

I add another moment to my collection as I hold him, wrapping my palms around the thick, hard length, fingertips tracing a dirty song over him. He makes a rough noise, but it's not enough. I want all of him. I lean closer and exhale, my chin bumping against his dick.

He groans. "Stop teasing, princess, and open up."

I glance up at him through my lashes, letting him see the laughter and lo—no, the *pleasure* I have in doing this for him. With him. Each memory that I'm adding to an ever-growing string of favorite moments. This. Kissing him, touching him, adding a different kind of pearl necklace to my dirty collection… I want it.

I want him.

I press my lips against him and he freezes. There's nothing between us and if it feels good to me, it must feel even better for him. The rough curse he lets loose when I rub my cheek against him seems like a good sign. So I make him mine. I kiss my way down and then up, curling my tongue around the head, then sucking him like he's my lollipop. He really likes that—the cursing picks up volume and he shoves his hands farther into my hair.

Despite being on my knees, his hands fisting my ponytail and guiding my head, this doesn't feel like some kind of power play. I'm tight with desire—to come, to please him, to be his in any way I can. And while I'm tempted to slip into the water just in case anyone does come by, I also want to give him this. To trust him. To make this good for him, too.

"Harper," he groans roughly, and when I struggle to take him all, to relax and let him in, I see how much he wants this. Me. *Us*. He's so goddamned big that I have serious doubts about handling this, but I take him anyhow. I relax until my mouth's stretched wide and he's hitting the back of my throat.

He tugs on my hair and I look up. "Okay?" he asks.

I hum a little note of agreement and he groans.

"Fuck, Harper. You're killing me."

He's discovered my secret master plan. I suck and moan, letting him know that we're in this together, letting his hands on my head guide me. He fucks my mouth deeper, faster, harder, and I move with him, cupping his balls and stroking.

He yanks my hair, the sharp sting waking an answering pulse between my legs. "Gonna come, Harper."

I nod around his dick. Yes. That's my plan.

He moves faster, I suck harder, and then he's grabbing my face, holding me still as he comes with a violent shudder. I swallow and then let him go.

"Jesus," he whispers roughly, scooping me up in his arms. "Harper."

He looks a little dazed and a whole lot possessive. Happy, too, which is funny when I think about it because as much as Vik's always laughing and joking, I'm not sure I'd describe him as *happy*. I'm not sure he ever lets down his guard enough to be that. Whatever he is, however, he's definitely mine.

"Good?" My gaze flips up to his and he nods.

"Your turn." There's a wealth of dirty promise in his voice as he wades into the water. The water is beyond icy, but it turns out that Vik knows exactly how to warm me up.

CHAPTER SIXTEEN

Harper

MY RELATIONSHIP WITH Vik feels as if it's shifted somehow, even though we're playing by the same set of rules as before. He always shows up when I text him for a booty call unless he has club business, but that's just sex. Super-amazing, sometimes dirty, but always wonderful sex. I love the sex. And I trust Vik. But it still seems weird, although that's probably my inner good girl making a token protest. *She's* never had hookup sex before, so she just needs to practice some more and then everything will be fine.

God. The *practicing*.

Vik's the sexiest man I've ever met. Honestly, he's set the bar way too high for Mr. Right. Creativity, stamina and a dirty mouth—Vik's bad-boy accessories are perfect. It's almost enough to make me redo the mental job description I've been carrying around for Mr. Right.

Almost. Not quite.

Because there are moments—not all that often,

but they happen—when it's impossible to forget that Vik's a biker. And while the commission of felonies may not be part of Vik's day-to-day, he has club brothers who've served or are serving time. No matter how many Toys for Tots drives they spearhead, the Hard Riders aren't firefighters, Boy Scouts or good-guy material. They're willing to break rules they dislike, and no matter how many marks fill the *plus* column, the number of negatives outweigh them. I'm still getting crap from my coworkers about my biker client, and not one but two of the firm's senior partners made a point of swinging by my office to "see how it's going." Convincing them I'm not laundering money for a drug cartel is harder than you'd think.

So tonight I'm focused on dating. Dating *other* men. Fine, upstanding, suit-wearing guys who have their eyes on a corner office and a home in the suburbs. I won't find Mr. Right if I don't get out there.

I steal a moment to text Vik and let him know about the night's plans. Reaching out to him, though, is a mistake. I can't think about him without remembering what he looked like naked in my bed, his clothes dropped on my floor. It kind of makes me want to invest in new furniture—maybe a four-poster bed I can tie him to spread-eagled. And since I have no plans to bring tonight's date home with me, I really should take care of business now.

Dating feels like I've just stepped into the biggest, baddest all-you-can-eat Vegas buffet—too many choices, a super-long line at the door and my table's *way* over in the corner. Tonight's guy seems like a good bet, though. Swipe right, tap the heart…and then wait to see if he'd done the same for me. He had, and now here I am, getting dressed for a date that feels kind of like cheating on Vik.

Obviously, I'll have to stop sleeping with him if it looks like there could be anything between me and Mr. Tinder. Vik's assured me that he understands, and that our hookups will remain private, but is it something I should tell tonight's date about?

How would I tell tonight's date? *Excuse me, but I've got this awesome friend with benefits who happens to be a badass biker. Oh. You want to know why I'm not seeing him?* Yeah. It's a good question, but I don't think we could have more, something besides the smoking-hot sex and the comfortable rides. We're friends, but I want a lover, and then eventually, I want a partner. Whoever he is, he'll be the kind of guy who will take Bing to the vet with me—not commit a felony to get him back.

And yet I want to go swimming together and barbecue again.

I want Vik full-time, instead of whichever hours he decides he can spare me, and that would mean changing the terms of our deal.

So I'm not really in a dating mood tonight.

I'm still in my yoga pants and an old Cornell T-shirt with no bra when there's a knock on the door followed by a text on my phone.

VIK: Open the door

I shouldn't, but I do. Vik's lounging against the frame, phone in one hand and a candy box tied up with a ridiculous pink-and-white bow in the other. He hands me the box and then gently nudges me out of his way. Of course I cave, and it has nothing to do with the fact that he's brought me my favorite sea salt caramels.

Vik tugs on the hem of my shirt. "Exactly where is Mr. Tinder taking you tonight?"

I shrug. "Dinner on the Strip."

To be honest, I haven't paid much attention to the details. Vik holds out his hand.

"Phone."

I hand it over and he looks up the texts I've exchanged with James the Lawyer. He grins at me. "You need a wardrobe change."

"You don't think this is dinner material?" I smooth a hand down my pants. I'm definitely not rocking a cocktail dress at the moment, and I do want to send the right message.

Vik smacks me gently on the butt. "Come on."

He heads for my bedroom, and I trail after him. It feels sort of weird, since we're not about to have sex, but if anyone knows what guys like, it's Vik. After all, he's dated pretty much everyone with a vagina in the greater Las Vegas area. When I catch up with him, he's already rummaging through my dresser drawers. Things have gotten far sexier—and skimpier— in those drawers since Vik and I hooked up. Case in point? The pale green thong Vik's currently admiring. That barely-there scrap of lace made a big impact on my credit card statement last month. It's too bad Victoria's Secret doesn't offer a travel points card because I'd have racked up enough to fly to Bora Bora and back by now.

It's weird to think that we could have had our last booty call. That if tonight works out, I won't be sleeping with Vik ever again. I don't believe in cheating and an open relationship isn't for me, and I suspect that Vik has the same set of no-cheating rules. For all that he's a lawless biker who probably commits felonies with casual nonchalance, he's got a streak of honor wider than the Grand Canyon.

He tosses the green thong onto my bed, and then rifles through my closet with the expertise of a Nordstrom personal shopper. Of course, watching his big hands move over my clothes just makes me want to suggest that we ax date night and strip instead. We could get naked, watch Sharknado movies together and take turns getting each other off. Or maybe whoever comes last gets to pick the next movie. That seems fair.

"Hey." He snaps his fingers gently. "We gotta get you dressed before Prince Charming shows up."

"You're really okay with this?" I automatically take the dress he hands me. It's an LBD—little black dress—and there's definitely no room in this Kate Spade number for a bra. The silky material hugs my hips but the top blouses gently, hiding all sorts of sins. There are worse choices.

Vik tugs on the satin ribbon that ties around my

neck, checking out my tag. "You and Kate should get married."

We tease back and forth, him making fun of my obsession with Kate Spade, me pointing out that there are more sartorial choices in this world than black T-shirts and jeans. It's fun. It's familiar—and I keep expecting him to go, to leave before my date arrives, but he shows no signs of departing. I'm trying to figure out how to give him the boot when there's a knock on the door.

"Showtime." Vik rubs his hands together as he bounces toward the door.

"Hey," I hiss, grabbing the hem of his T-shirt. "What do you think you're doing?"

"Getting the door." He flashes me an innocent smile. "You should thank me for being so helpful."

"I think you're leaving," I say firmly. No point in beating around the bush—subtlety is wasted on Vik.

"So I'm headed in the right direction." His grin widens.

I elbow him out of the way and make it to the door first. I don't need tonight's date scared off before we even make it to the lobby. Vik grunts but lets me open the door.

The guy on the other side looks exactly like his Tinder picture. His navy blue suit is expensive but not flashy, as are the Ferragamo loafers. He's skipped the tie but gone for a dress shirt open at the throat. The whole effect is very similar to one of those gorgeous, slick Christmas presents you pay to have gift wrapped at Macy's.

"Hi. Harper, I assume?" He leans in and brushes a quick kiss over my cheek rather than sticking out his hand. Jeez. He'd better hope he has the right girl. I can't help but notice that we're the same height. In fact, with my heels I might have an inch on him.

"Nice to meet you, James." I beam determinedly at him and nod like a bobblehead as I step backward so he can come in. Bar meetings are less awkward and I make a mental note for next time. The odds of my finding Mr. Right on my first date are low, so I should learn from tonight's mistakes so I can get it right next time. *Kill me.*

Vik materializes behind my shoulder. He doesn't even try to be sneaky about it—he just stomps right up. James looks slightly concerned.

"Is this your brother?"

Vik snorts. "I'm her best friend."

Huh. That doesn't sound half as crazy as it should.

James looks a little uncertain but game. "Okay, then."

Vik leans against the wall, crossing his arms over his chest and pretty much blocking the entire hallway. "And where are you taking our Harper tonight, James?"

Unless he was hit by the amnesia stick in the last five minutes, Vik knows exactly where we're headed.

"I have reservations for us at Picasso."

Vik nods. "Harper likes the fountain. You want to show her a good time, you make sure she can see it, you feel me? Pretty fucking romantic watching the show."

"Hey." I'm pretty sure my face is moving from peony pink to flaming tomato red. Best friend does *not* mean Vik gets to act like my dad. "I can manage my own date."

Vik doesn't get the hint. "She likes shellfish. Steak so raw you think it's gonna fucking moo at you. Anything with truffles in it or sugar on it."

James smiles, and it's a nice smile. The corners of his mouth curve right up, the smile reaching his eyes. He's decided this is funny, and I can't really blame him. I'm starting to suspect that Vik would wrap me in a chastity belt if he had one handy.

"We'll get the biggest lobsters in Vegas," he promises easily. "Are we ready?"

Vik shoves off the wall. "How are you getting there?"

Jeez. "Vik—"

He holds up a hand. "Let the man answer the question, Harper."

"My car's out front," James says. "Mercedes-Benz C-Class. The National Highway Traffic Safety Administration promises Harper will be safe with me. It's got one of the best ratings for crashes."

"Are you planning on crashing tonight?"

Wisely, James starts heading for the door.

I follow him, snagging my purse from the side table. "We're done here."

Vik ignores me. "Harper's fucking priceless. You treat her like that, you feel me?"

"Absolutely." James pulls the door open and waits for me to go first. God. He's such a gentleman.

"Thanks for having this conversation with me." Vik slaps James on the back. We're all bottled up at the door, and I'm starting to get concerned that I might never get to head out on my date (at least not without a bonus biker chaperone) when Vik's phone rings.

That's his dad's ringtone.

"What's up?" he asks as he steps away.

"Are you ready?" James presses his hand against the small of my back and my new firebird, urging me toward the door. He's right. We should totally take advantage of Vik's distraction to escape. I'm sure we've got reservations and shouldn't be late, but something's up from the way Vik's free hand taps out an impatient rhythm against his thigh. I can't hear much but I know that Mr. Serge isn't in the best of health, physically or mentally, and Vik worries.

"Is everything okay?" I wait for Vik to hang up and follow us out before locking up. James moves down the hall ahead of us, punching the button for the elevator and generally giving us some space.

Vik shakes his head. "My dad's had some kind of thing. Don't know what, but Lora's driving him to the ER because he's refusing an ambulance. She says it's probably just heartburn, but we should be sure. I'm gonna go meet them."

"I can go with you."

"I've got this. You go on your date." He pauses, and for a moment I think he might kiss me—or pull me into a hug. We're friends. It would be okay. Instead after a few awkward seconds, he shoots me a careful smile and lopes toward the stairwell.

"See you," he calls over his shoulder.

So I go. I mean, what else can I do? And it turns out fine. Fine but boring. James doesn't have tattoos, doesn't ride balls-out, but he also doesn't judge me. Or fuck me up against a wall, kiss me senseless, make me laugh.

Turns out, a guy can wear a suit and still be Mr. All Wrong.

CHAPTER SEVENTEEN

Harper

VIK'S NOT MY loaner penis.

Okay.

He's not *just* my loaner penis.

He's not *just* anything. How do I know this? Let me count the ways. Item one: I'm reading his texts while I mainline my sad desk salad at work. Usually, I do a quick run-through of the major financial news sites while I work my way through two cups of arugula and a can of dolphin-safe tuna fish. Item two? I spent the weekend texting him and trying *not* to run over to his place to check up on him.

I'm not sure how his dad is doing, or if Vik's okay. He spent the weekend with his dad, which I totally get. The Friday-night ER visit turned out to be precautionary rather than required, and his dad's back home. Vik is still trying to sort out tests and doctors, but he claims everything is more or less fine. I'm not so convinced, even though today's text has me smiling, and it's not even funny. Or dirty. Or *unusual*.

And that's the problem right there.

My phone always starts buzzing at 12:01 because he knows I'll ignore him before I take my solo thirty minutes. At 12:01, however, he'll text What r u doing? and I'll text back. That's how our Mondays go. There are limits, of course, on the shareable stuff. I don't give him details about my trades or the investments I've set up; I don't tell him dollar amounts, names or personally identifying information. We're just swapping stories. He knows about Coffee Man, who never comes in without two Americanos clutched in his hands, and who gets progressively more jittery as our half-hour appointment winds to a close because it's time for his next hit. He laughs his ass off at It Girl, whose portfolio is entirely invested in the fashion industry—and who picks her stocks based on the contents of her closet. He tells me to give Weeping Widow a hug (which I can't, although she really needs it) when she dissolves into tears yet again because I want her to make changes to the investments her husband set up and she wants everything to stay the same even though it's already changed.

Sure enough, my phone buzzes with Vik's favorite question. What r we eating today?

I'm not adventurous when it comes to food. My standard Monday fare is arugula, tuna and feta. For 358 calories, I get 39 grams of protein and 2 measly grams of fiber. I went wild this morning and added a cup of blueberries because fruit is good for me and you can't have too much vitamin C and folate in your life. I send Vik a picture even though my Tupperware

hardly qualifies as food porn. Vik promptly counters with a picture of the taco truck parked outside
Ink Me.

There's only one response besides demanding he
run a bag of that goodness over here. I can hear your
arteries clogging from over here.

I've offered to make him a salad to take to work.
His whereabouts are unpredictable, I've pointed out.
There's zero guarantee he finds a food truck because
he's not always at Ink Me. He doesn't share details
about Hard Rider business, but he's frequently on
the road on his bike or out at the clubhouse. There
are things he can't tell me, just like there are things I
can't tell him. I suspect the key difference is that his
things could get him five to ten years in state prison.

We eat lunch together over our phones, texting
back and forth. When I ask about his morning, he
bitches about a rainbow and unicorn tattoo requested
by a college freshman.

Don't want to talk about that. U got ur next ink picked
out?

I suddenly know how Eve felt when the serpent
started pitching his suggestions. No, I haven't thought
about getting more ink. In fact, I'm still kind of getting used to the newly healed firebird on my back
because it's my first, it was a drunken impulse and
neither of those things gets much play in my life. But
maybe I *should* think about getting more. If the first

was so amazing, how much better will the second one be? Or the third?

I can haz rainbow kitten?

Google produces a truly astonishing number of rainbow-colored kitten images, and I send him a selection. You know. Just to torture him. His response is short and to the point.

Fuck no.

Alrighty then. This would be more fun if I could see his face, but I'll just have to make do.

What would you ink if it were your skin?

He fires back an answer quickly.

Kinda think it is my skin

Huh. That's not disturbing at all.

Brooklyn bangs on my door while I'm still trying to decide how I feel about Vik's inner caveman coming out to play. After I sad-desk-salad and text with Vik for thirty minutes, she and I speed walk around the block half a dozen times. Otherwise, as she's pointed out, we only get up to pee and we hobble like we're eighty. The mile we squeeze in also burns off approximately a dozen lettuce leaves and several bonus blueberries. It's a win-win.

I snap the lid onto my Tupperware, de-mute my phone and follow her outside, squinting. I usually don't see so much sunlight on a weekday. Good thing Kate's got my back with a pair of snazzy sunglasses.

I'm barely outside, however, when my phone goes off, Marvin Gaye's "Let's Get It On" announcing an incoming text from Vik. I should have stayed muted even if I am temporarily out of the office.

"Haaaarper." Brooklyn draws the syllables of my name out.

I concentrate on focusing straight ahead and resist the urge to yank my phone out and see what Vik's said this time.

Undeterred, Brooklyn pokes me in the side. "Is it your pet Viking? Show me."

Ever since Vik sent me a shirtless selfie (his jeans were partially undone as well for added biker badness), Brooklyn has hounded me to share. She claims it's selfish to keep all that hotness to myself.

Brooklyn makes a give-it-up gesture. "Is he wearing the boots today?"

We both take a moment to mentally appreciate the goodness that is Vik in a pair of motorcycle boots.

My phone announces a second new text.

I should get that. I'm sure I need another half-naked selfie from Vik like I need a hole in the head, but screw it. He's gorgeous, I'm weak and hearing from him sort of makes my day. I pull my phone out and we both stop walking, cupping our hands over the screen to see better.

It's a picture of his…stomach. Okay. It's *way* better than it sounds because the man's six-pack hosts its own eight-pack and that much smooth, hard, muscled man begs a girl to lick and touch. Obviously, I need to get a grip, but still.

Brooklyn lets out a little moan of appreciation, and I fight the urge to do a triumphant fist pump. That's *my* man.

Wait.

Rewind.

When did he become *mine*? Because he's totally, absolutely not and any unrequired liking or possessiveness on my part will end badly.

"You're so lucky." Brooklyn's finger hovers over the screen. "You've totally won the boyfriend sweepstakes. Send this to me? Just, you know, so I have something droolworthy for my screensaver?"

"We're not—"

Shut *up*. I start walking. God, I'm in so much trouble.

"Not what?" The mischievous smile curling the edges of Brooklyn's mouth warns me that I'm about to be given so much shit it would take me a month to shovel it. Hercules could clean up a dozen Augean stables in the time I'd need to deal with what Brooklyn's about to land on me.

"Not boyfriend/girlfriend," I grit out.

There's a brief moment of silence broken only by the usual cacophony of Vegas traffic (so okay, it's still really freaking noisy but *Brooklyn* stays quiet), and then she positively cackles.

"How's the weather in the Land of de Nile?" she

asks. "Is it hot enough for you? Because the two of you are a thing. An item. The world's dirtiest and most ill-kept secret."

"We have sex. Nothing wrong with that."

I sneak another peek at the picture he's sent me. He's sprawled in a chair, the phone angled away to take the shot of his stomach. I've got some bonus blue jeans (those buttons are my favorite) and...there's a rainbow-colored kitten cavorting with his belly button. The man definitely shouldn't be left alone with Sharpies.

"Harper." Brooklyn's voice is soft but insistent. "If you're not dating, what are the two of you doing?"

I shove my phone back into my pocket. "Hooking up."

"Uh-huh."

I'm not sure which of us sounds less certain—me or Brooklyn. And she's got a point. No matter how hard I try to spin it, Vik's not just my loaner penis providing physical release. Our hookup is becoming something more...something way too much like an emotional connection for my comfort.

CHAPTER EIGHTEEN

Harper

BROOKLYN'S WORDS STICK with me for the rest of the day. And then the next day and the next day after that. In fact, they hang around the entire week and take up permanent residence in my head. What's up between me and Vik? I'd like to pretend that I don't know, but it doesn't take much thinking to figure out. I'm falling for him.

I'm falling in love with my fuck buddy.

With my best friend.

With Vik.

Our deal was sex with no strings, a hot hookup when we were in the mood and lonely. I should have stopped as soon as *lonely* turned into *loving* for me. Vik doesn't want my feelings. And honestly? I don't want them, either. They'll spoil everything. Vik has been clear from the start that he's all fun and no feelings. When it comes to saying three little words, he'll always choose *on your knees* over *I love you*.

So when he hits my place on Friday night, I open

the door for him. I pretend nothing has changed and everything's perfectly fine. My feelings are my dirty little secret. I'll pretend I'm looking for Mr. Right when it turns out I've been holding him all along. And if my heart gets broken or trampled beneath a pair of too-sexy motorcycle boots, that's my problem.

I make it through the ten cartons of Chinese take-out that Vik adores. I make it through two hours and twelve minutes of the fourth Pirates of the Caribbean movie. And then in minute two hundred and thirteen, I lose it. Jack's cupping Angelica's face and he's finally giving it up, admitting he loves her, and it's so goddamned romantic and yet it's also about to be over. The shooting-each-other and fighting stuff isn't long-term relationship material and Angelica clearly has commitment issues, but I want them to just kiss and shut up. Kiss and be happy. Kiss and sail off into the sunset together to create baby pirates and major mayhem together.

Instead, they part.

"Hey." Vik nudges me. "You okay, babe?"

No. No, I am not. I want to crawl on top of him, wrap my arms around his neck and hang on like a love-deprived baby monkey. I want to stick to him, hold him, wrap myself around him like there's no tomorrow because it sucks to realize that tomorrow might have to happen without him and that I want so much more than sex from this man.

"I can't—"

The words get stuck in my throat. I should tell him that we're over. That I can't fuck my best friend anymore because it feels wrong. Because I've gotten too close and he hasn't gotten close enough.

"Hey." He brushes a thumb over my wet cheek. "What's wrong?"

"Nothing," I say, meaning it. I feel everything, and he feels nothing.

He grabs the remote and hits the power button. Jack's boat disappears as Vik frowns at me.

"Work too much this week?"

Now is not the moment for emotional revelations. Plus, I hate crying. Tears fix nothing; plans are far more effective. Unfortunately, there's no plan to make Vik fall in love with me.

"Maybe we shouldn't do this anymore."

He tosses the remote onto the coffee table. "Do what?"

"Us. Hooking up."

We're sitting in the dark because Vik insists movie-watching must be done in total blackness, so I can't see his face. But I feel him move. He scoops me up like I'm a delicate flower and then he's carrying me to the bedroom. Even when he sets me down on the mattress, I can't turn the stupid tears off.

He hesitates. I know he doesn't know what to do. I never cry, and we're all about having fun anyhow. We laugh together, but the sadder stuff is off-limits. He wouldn't let me in when his dad had that episode, and he's never deliberately let me see him when he was feeling down or vulnerable or anything other than him being a badass and rocking life. And I've kind of been the same way.

He doesn't say anything, but then he follows me down onto the bed, his arms hold me tight, making promises. I'm safe. He's here. If anything needs to be killed or hurt, he's the man to do it. And his mouth…

His mouth kisses away my tears.

He doesn't give me words, but he gives me everything else. He doesn't tell me not to cry. He doesn't ask why. He just holds me, and I can almost pretend that it feels like something. Like he loves me. Like he really, truly is my best friend and my partner and that he's got me. That the heart beating so steadily beneath my folded hands is mine. *Stupid.*

When the tears start to dry up, he kisses the corner of my mouth. And then my mouth. It's a soft kiss, his lips closed, just brushing mine. Letting me know he's here, too, and that I'm not alone. I could get used to kisses like his. Curled up together as we are, however, it's impossible to miss the way his dick tents the front of his jeans, big and hard. Demanding attention.

"Ignore him," Vik says roughly. "He's got no sense of timing, you feel me?"

Happy to oblige, I slide my hand from his heart to his dick because that's what we have, and I want one last time, one last set of memories. If I can't have forever, I'm stealing right now.

"Make love to me." I try not to cringe as the words leave my mouth. He's so big, so gorgeous and so distant. He nods slowly, but I know he thinks my request is just girl wording. That I'm really asking him to fuck or screw or bang me and not for anything more. He'd panic if he knew I loved him.

"You sure this is what you want to do?"

"I am. I do."

He looks down at me, his hands cupping my face. The kiss he gives me is sweet and quick, his lips barely skating across mine. I lift up, chasing his mouth with mine, and he chuckles. Bastard. Stupid, fucking, wonderful, not-mine bastard.

"You got it." He comes down over me, planting his knees on either side of my hips. We're face-to-face, but his mouth is too far away from mine. The handful of inches separating us is wider than the Grand Canyon.

I tug on his T-shirt. "Get naked."

"As you wish." His grin flashes in the darkness.

He looks happier now that the waterworks have dried up and we're back on familiar ground. And me? I want whatever he'll give me, which likely makes me pathetic. I need his skin on mine, nothing between us. He sits back, hauling the shirt over his head, and I watch his big hands work.

The shirt hits the floor, leaving him bare-chested. God, I love his chest. It's all sexy muscles and tempting ridges that ripple with power as he twists to consider his boots. Yeah. Those boots are a problem.

"Be right back." He brushes another kiss over my mouth and then rolls off me. He makes short work of stripping off the rest of his clothes and then he removes mine. He drops carefully back down on top of me.

I spread my legs, making room for him, and wrap my arms around him. And for a moment I hang on. I let myself forget that eventually we'll get up and go about our lives and I won't get to keep him.

"In." I reach between us, going straight for his dick.

His forehead creases. "Condom would be a good idea, babe."

"I'm on the pill." Since condoms are only 75 percent effective, I'm on the pill. Still, we've always used a condom. I've never given him the go-ahead to take me bare. I want to be his first for something.

He hesitates. "Let me touch you."

"Now," I insist. I don't want foreplay, not tonight. I don't want him to drive me any crazier for him. I just want to feel connected to him.

He pushes slowly inside me and I can feel my body opening for him. I don't think we've ever gone slow, and yet it's so good like this. Quieter, softer, but still good. Instead of chasing my orgasm, I just feel him becoming part of me. I feel his thrusts become deeper and harder, his hips slapping softly against mine as he grunts something that might be my name. I think he needs this, too.

"I love you." The words slip out of my mouth, and I don't hold them back. I need to say them. I need him to hear me.

"Harper." He freezes above me.

"I love you." It's the least I can say, and it doesn't feel like enough. Or too much because he's shaking his head.

"You don't love me. You love this."

And then he leans down and kisses me, cutting off the words. His kiss is rough and wet, raw and carnal. His teeth nip, demanding I open up, and then he thrusts inside my mouth, his tongue fucking me to the rhythm of his dick. He rolls, pulling me on top of him so that I'm riding him, his dick shoved deep inside me. Big hands cup my butt, working me against him in a dirty, sexy rhythm. I brace my hands on his chest, leaning down into him, because he's the only solid thing in my universe now, and then he gives it to me hard.

He slams up into me where I'm tight and hot and aching for him, making me gasp as he pushes inside until he bottoms out and there's no more room. I tighten around him, holding on. He doesn't get to leave me. Not yet.

He pulls back. Thrusts into me again.

Heat and fire explode through me, my body going ballistic. It loves dirty sex. It loves this man. He pinches my clit, his devilish fingers circling and teasing until I can't hold back any longer. He's watching me when I come, and because he may own my heart but he doesn't own my mouth or my head or anything else other than that stupid, stupid organ, I tell him the truth he can't fuck out of me.

"I love you."

CHAPTER NINETEEN

Vik

WHAT THE FUCK does Harper mean?

I love you.

We had a deal and nowhere in our discussion of friends with benefits and sexy hookups was love mentioned. The whole faux boyfriend/girlfriend was just to make my old man happy. But right now my dick's in control, and he wants to come, so come we do. I hammer into the sweet, slick pussy clenching around me, and try not to think. The tightness in my balls is all the feeling I need, fuck her very much.

She was looking for a long-term guy. I helped her scope out dates. I practically *gave* her away. *Goddamn it.*

I'm balls-deep in her and she's stripped away more than just the condom. I have no idea what to do next, so I make her come. I touch and tease until she stops shouting *I love you* and makes those cute but indecipherable whimpering noises that herald her orgasm. And afterward, I may sort of pull her close. I mean, we've reestablished our boundaries, right? When she said those words, it was probably just the sex talking. Or hormones. Pheromones. Something.

She rests her cheek against my chest, breathing hard. I probably qualify for bastard of the year, if we're being honest. She cried, and I fucked her. Cowgirl style. The only feelings allowed here are of the orgasmic, blissful kind. I know I'm an idiot for passing on the possibility of something more but that's me. An idiot. No way anything else could work out between us anyhow. It's not like I'm a white-picket-fence kind of guy—or the kind of man she can dress up in a suit and take to her company cocktail parties. I do dirty sex and I do it well. Really, really fucking well. Feelings, however, are not part of our deal.

The sounds of Bon Jovi's "Ride Cowboy Ride" fill the air.

"That's your dad," Harper says. I both hate and love how she knows that I've given my dad that Bon Jovi ringtone. It makes it harder to pretend that we're just sex and nothing else.

I grab my phone from the pile of clothes on the floor and answer. Apparently, it's my night for crying women.

It's Lora on the other end. At least, I think it's Lora. The number's right, but she's crying so hard I'm not certain. Could be some random stranger sobbing into my ear.

"Calm the fuck down." Harper stiffens by my side. Think she's about to rip me a new one for my lack of manners, but then Lora spits out the words she's choking on.

"Your dad's dead."

I turn my phone off when I reach the hospital, and I don't fire it back up for two days. There's no club business that needs me; Prez knows where I am and that I have personal biz. By the time my old man's been gone two days, however, I decide it's time to stop being such a pussy. I turn my phone back on, and watch the screen blow up with messages.

Stupid.

I delete the voice mails straight off. Nothing I need to hear there. The texts are harder. Got plenty from my brothers, reaching out and asking me if I need anything. As if. The practical stuff is harder. I deal with the doctors, the hospital, the funeral home and Lora. Shitload of other people come out of the wood-work, too, needing decisions about this, that and the other thing. And then there's Harper. She must spend every free moment she has texting me because my phone's at 317 messages and counting. The 317th is a fucking doozy—she's been threatening since 246 to track me down and verify for herself that I'm okay. Not that she thinks I am—that's clear. But that's what losing your old man does to you. I get through the first night by shacking up with Jack Daniels, mostly because I'm dumb as shit. Each swallow dulls the memories a little more, but it all comes crashing back in the morning with a souvenir killer headache.

I know Harper and I have unresolved shit, but I'm

in no mood to talk. Whenever I think about her, something twists inside of me. That call could have been
about her. The closer someone gets, the more it fucking burns when they go away. By the time my phone
lights up with message 318, I'm feeling really fucking sorry for myself.

HARPER: When's the funeral? I want to be there
for you.

ME: Not necessary.

HARPER: I want to.

Life's funny—we don't always get what we want.
Santa Claus isn't real, and he doesn't give a boo-
fucking-hoo about hitting the highlights on Harper's
wish list. I don't know what's happening between us
right now—other than me avoiding the shit out of
her—but I'm telling myself that the only *wants* I've
got are sexual. Got a whole list of preferred positions
and dirty fantasies she and I haven't worked out yet.
The dirty dangle, doing it accordion style, the electric
slide…plenty of shit we haven't tried. Or we could just
redo a few favorites. She fucking mewls like a kitten when I do her hard from behind—I love that, too.
  So what the fuck does she think I need from her
right now? I'm not sure what I'm supposed to say.
Yeah, come hold my hand because I need…what?
We're just a hookup. Can't afford to be more. My
fingers fly across my phone with a life of their own.

ME: I don't need a girlfriend.

My stupid, stupid fingers.

Harper doesn't text me anymore after that.

I don't bury my old man alone.

My brothers have my back. My dad might not have patched into our club, but he rode and he was mine, and by extension that means he's theirs. Too many fucking pronouns in that mix, but you feel me. Don't need their interference in my life, but it feels good to know that they care.

"You ready to do this?" Prez straddles his bike, hands on his thighs. Could be out for just any ride, but for the black bandanna around his upper arm.

"Yeah," I say, throwing a leg over my own bike. "Time to let him fly."

He nods slowly. "Okay to hold on, though, if that's what you want."

Doesn't matter what I want so goddamned bad because my old man's dead. I won't turn around and find him riding my ass, a grin lighting up his face because he knows he's got me. Old man loved to get a rise out of me. Might have fought over it, but I loved him.

"Let's ride."

"No one else we're waiting for?"

I make a show of looking around the parking lot. "Entire fucking club's here. You think I shoulda hired a brass band, too?"

Prez shakes his head. "Your girl not coming?"

"We covered this before. I don't have a girl."

Prez grunts. "You ask her to come?"

"None of her business," I say slowly. "She's not a biker, doesn't ride with our club. Got no place for her here."

Prez looks over at Romeo. "Jesus, he's stupid."

Romeo's nodding hard enough to fall off his bike. "You fuck it up with her?"

"You ever know me to have a long-term relationship?"

"The kind where you fuck the same woman more than twice and wake up in her bed?" Romeo asks me.

"Sure."

Prez looks me over. "He did."

"Some shit's off-limits," I say. No big surprise that they fucking keep right on talking. My brothers are worse than a bunch of girls when it comes to this feelings business. Must have some of that attitude written on my face because Prez hooks a finger in my vest and pulls me close, dropping a heavy arm around my shoulder. Fucking feels like the man's made out of iron.

"You think there's no place for a woman in this club?" he asks. "Because you take a good look around you. Some of our brothers, they've found themselves an old lady and they've been smart enough to hang on. Put themselves the fuck out there and get down on their knees if that's what it takes to make her stay. And if you think that's a weakness, you're dumber than I think. Those old ladies are the heart of this club, so that makes them the best fucking part of us. Sometimes it's easier to do your thinking with your dick, but they make us more. Make us better."

"Didn't know it was national poetry day. Don't see you wearing any old lady arm candy."

Prez cuffs my head hard. "Just because shit's sweet doesn't make it candy. You find an old lady, you do whatever you need to do to keep her. If fate drops someone into my lap, I'm gonna throw an arm around her and hold her tight. Not ashamed to admit that there can be more than a quick fuck. Sometimes, you meet someone who belongs by your side and at your back, not just under you."

"She's not my old lady," I say.

Not about to share my sex life with my club president. It's none of the club's business, and I'm not a porn channel he can surf. Sex with Harper was amazing. It's just that…Harper's looking for that shit, too. She wants forever and family and a goddamned dozen qualities I can never be for her, and not just because I don't own a suit. Some brothers settle down, while the rest of us ride on.

"Hear you," Prez says slowly. "Not a question of what she is now—because the answer to that would be *not fucking here*. More interested in what she could be if you were man enough to let her."

"Yeah, well, what if I don't want an old lady?"

"Jesus," Romeo mutters. "You don't want to win the lottery, either?"

Harper would not only know the odds on winning the lottery, but she'd know what came next, too. She never could wrap her head around my old man's love of scratch-off tickets. Said it would be just as effective to burn your dollar or use it as toilet paper. Plus, she'd trotted out all sorts of sad sack stories about winners who went bust or ended up worse off than before because a lottery win's a onetime thing and not an evergreen money tree you plant in your backyard.

"Harper and me are over," I tell them.

Prez mimes shooting himself in the head. "Stupid as fuck."

On that we're agreed.

It's time to ride, though, and so Prez stands up on the seat of his bike, hand balanced on Romeo's head. The rest of the club immediately shuts the fuck up.

"We're gonna say goodbye to a good brother today," he says. He adds a few sentences about who my old man had been, his service to his country and how he and Prez had met. They're good words, but I'm itching to ride.

My brothers listen, heads bowed in respect. Planting my old man in the ground had seemed too much like tying him down, so I'd had the body cremated. We'd let him ride, fly free over the highway he'd raced down so many times. I wait for the familiar stab of pain, and sure enough it comes. We'd had our differences, but we'd had our good moments, too.

We hit the highway at sunset, going balls-out as the desert stretches away from us on either side. It's a good night for a ride, and when we crest a little rise in the highway, I know it's time. I pop the lid on my old man's urn and hold it overhead, letting what's left of him fly free. Might be some people who think this is disrespectful, but he loved the road and the desert. He was happiest here, so this is the right spot to send him on ahead of us on his next ride. Someday sooner or later I'll catch up with him, and he'll give me shit for screwing things up with Harper.

I can't wait to see him again.

CHAPTER TWENTY

Harper

I'M SITTING OUTSIDE Vik's place having a painful moment of personal reflection that *Cosmo* promises will bring 100 percent personal growth, but which makes me think the universe is one sadistic bitch. Yes, I've come looking for Vik. No, he didn't ask me to be here. I'm torn between labeling this a gutsy all-in move on my part and recognizing that it smacks of desperation. I know he laid his father to rest today, or tried to. Not one but four bikers texted me. I want to be here for him in case he needs anything, but I've also been sitting outside long enough to realize a few things. The most important revelation is that I don't have a key to his place. I have free access to his dick but not to his front door.

And if I need any confirmation that today's been rough, he arrives in a truck. In the passenger-side seat. Vik hates letting anyone else drive, so he must be half-wasted. The biker doing the driving helps him out, shoving a broad shoulder underneath Vik's arm so he can steer him toward the front door.

"I'm unavailable tonight," Vik announces, bracing his forearm against the door. His voice is a liquid, drunken slur.

"You're unavailable every night," I point out.

Biker buddy just kind of shakes his head. He's built like a mountain, which appears to be a requirement for joining the Hard Riders, and his long blond hair has been pulled back in a thick tail and braided. He's got ink on his forearms, more on his throat, and I'm pretty sure that if I patted him down for weapons, I'd uncover a small arsenal. And yet despite the aura of danger he projects, he gives me a polite tip of his head.

"I'm taking over." I squint (no glasses tonight) to read the patch on his vest. *Romeo.* I hope the story behind his road name is happier than the original.

Romeo doesn't let go until he's wrestled Vik inside and Vik's not only heavy as a bear, but he's also distinctly uncooperative. He bitches and mutters profanities while Romeo sort of accidentally elbows him in the stomach and then transfers him into my custody when we're by the side of the couch. I score a head tip and then Romeo hightails it out the door. Smart man.

This is the point at which I run out of plan. My dress is a black-and-white-striped A-line number with a scoop neck. It stops an inch above my knee. I look cute—and all wrong. Black's the color for funerals, and he doesn't need *cute*. Not now.

"Why are you here?" he asks.

"Holding you up." To prove my point, I let go, and Vik promptly face-plants onto the sofa. "Or letting you go. Take your pick."

He rolls over onto his back, glaring at me. "Did you come here for this?"

This is the monster dick he cups through his jeans.

"I came here for you. You're more than just—*we're* more than just—sex." I drag my eyes back up to his face, needing him to understand. He looks so sad, and I want so badly to fix that.

"No. We're not." He yanks open his jeans and fists himself. He's hard. I'm not sure if I should be flattered or concerned.

And it's totally wrong, but I'm turned on. The adrenaline pumping through me from our almost-fight is heating me up in more ways than one. Or maybe it's because the more I watch him treat his dick like it's the world's greatest plaything, the angrier I get. We may have started as a booty call, but we've moved on. We're definitely something more, even if he doesn't want to hear anything I've got to say. On a scale of one to ten, our emotions are running at twenty, but even if he won't talk to me, maybe I can reach out to him this way. I know it sounds stupid, but that's my plan. I step closer and lean toward him.

"You're in my space," he growls, his hand moving faster. He's going to come without me, and I refuse to be left behind.

"Goddamned straight I am."

I slide my hand up his arm and cup the back of his neck. He doesn't pull away, so that's a green light, right? Plus, his dick is all but stabbing me in the stomach as he continues to work himself with his palm. New plan. I'll kiss that angry look right off his face. I yank his face to mine.

He tastes like the whiskey he's poured down his throat tonight. He tastes like Vik. I kiss him with everything I have until he yanks his head back from mine.

"Leave." The word comes out hoarse and rasping, like he's fighting for air. My own breathing sounds like a freight train, a heavy, panting whine. I need him so badly.

"Bedroom," I snap. "Now."

He gives me a look I can't interpret. Anger, need, rage, possibly homicidal intentions. And then he moves so fast I don't see him coming. He jerks me off my feet, and I'm flying through the air, a completely undignified shriek leaving my mouth. I land hard on Vik's shoulder with a loud whoosh.

"You don't get to give me orders," he snarls. "Not today, not ever. We clear on that?"

"Crystal," I snap in my best Colonel Jessup imitation, jamming the heels of my hands into the small of his back. Don't think Vik likes it because he smacks my butt with his palm. We've done dirty things together, but spanking isn't one of them and I don't think he's playing tonight. How can this be the same man I've held and loved? The laughing man is gone, replaced by a surly-tempered giant with a raging hard-on.

At least the hard-on is familiar. He storms down

the hallway to his bedroom, ignoring my attempts to spank *his* ass and see how he likes it. What happens next is equally familiar. He tosses me onto the bed and shoves his jeans down. Naked, pissed-off Vik is definitely worth looking at. This has to be why I'm not scrambling off the bed and sprinting for the door. The wide-open, not-locked, I-could-totally-leave-through-it door.

"Clothes off," he says, voice hard. "Or get the hell out. Your choice."

"Why?" I must have lost my ever-loving mind because now I'm just taunting him.

"Because I want to have sex with you."

Definitely crystal clear.

"Never mind," he says, and reaches for me. Arousal mixes with a sudden dose of adrenaline. He's my Vik, and yet he's not. He spins me around before I can figure it out and flips up my dress. Hooking a finger in my panties, he tugs them down.

I twist, trying to see his face, but his weight pressing against me on the bed like he's done so many times before. My heartbeat pounds in my ears, but the wave of heat that tears through me drowns out everything else. I may moan. I'm entirely certain I moan. This isn't what I planned but if it's the only way he'll let me get close, I'll take it.

He rolls forward, his weight pushing me deeper into the bed. His dick slides between my butt cheeks and I tense. He's huge, and while so far angry sex is checking all my boxes, other things remain firmly in

my no-fly zone. Like butt sex. I make an embarrassing squeaking sound and he laughs.

"I could make you like it."

He makes the dirtiest, most beautiful promises,
but kink isn't what I want right now.

"Not tonight."

If I have my way, we'll have plenty of tomorrows to
explore what each of us likes or dislikes. Vik brushes
a finger over my tight pucker. And he's right. It does
feel good, all that heat and need prickling through
me as I grind my hips into his mattress.

I twist my head, pressing my lips against his. If he
doesn't want to talk, we won't. His beautiful, sulky
mouth has a fresh bruise at the corner. He's been
fighting, and he's been hurt enough. I nip, harder than
I should. He grunts, deepening both our kiss and his
caress as his hand rubs my butt again, sliding back up
between my cheeks and pressing against my pucker.
Barely touching me, but I know what it feels like
when the big, bad wolf comes knocking at my door.

Good.

It feels good.

"Do you like that?" He rubs his erection against
my butt. *That* is a little vague, and we're in unfamiliar territory, but I've always liked everything Vik has
done to me. With me. For me. I nod enthusiastically
and he taps the back of my thighs.

"Open up. I'll make you feel better."

My knees know who they trust. Unlike my head,
they don't need to think shit over or come up with a

plan. They part slowly, but they hold nothing back. They let him have everything and anything.

A fingertip traces the seam of my folds, teasing. I whimper, trying to force him deeper. Vik's such a gentleman, because he dips his finger deeper and then strokes slowly up. Down. Everywhere he touches me I'm hot and wet, my body aching, begging for more. The tension builds, my body taking over because I'm about to come and I'm right here, bent over Vik's bed and on the edge of falling off into the world's biggest orgasm ever and—

He stops.

"If you didn't come here for sex, you don't need this," he growls.

Logically, I know I can't die from not coming. Vik, however, is looking at a death sentence because I'm going to kill him.

"This night going according to plan, babe?"

He holds me still with an arm at the small of my back when I try to wriggle upright. He is such a bastard.

"I came here for you," I hiss. "Not a hookup."

"This is all I have to give you, babe."

I hesitate. "I want everything you have to give."

He's wrong. He's so much more than a talented set of fingers or a big dick. I need to tell him that, make him understand, but he grabs my hips and positions himself at my entrance.

God, he's huge.

And impatient.

He shoves himself deep inside me, driving home, and fuck words. I scream, letting everything I'm feeling out. Being facedown on Vik's bed helps with that—the sound's muffled and it's just him and me. It feels good and it feels raw and I don't want him to stop. He pounds into me, creating a raw burn that becomes the brightest, strongest pleasure ever. It's like the night we re-met and he inked me, the pain and discomfort becoming a doorway I step through to somewhere pleasurable. I'm making noises and he's grunting, his hips slapping against my ass with each hard stroke. Right now, he's all mine.

And like the pain when he inked me, my anger changes, becoming something else. It's a connection, a feeling, a heated, pissed-off, burning, fucking fantastic sensation that I refuse to feel guilty about because it's not PC. He pushes me open, slamming into me hard and with none of his usual finesse. It's as if everything inside him has burst open, too, and now he can't or won't hold back. My head hits the mattress with each rough stroke, my thighs bowed wide, and it's so impossibly good.

He comes first, holding me wide-open as he empties himself into me, stretching me so he can fill me up. I cry out because he can't leave me behind, not this time, not when it matters so much that we go somewhere, anywhere together. But fuck him. I can take what I want, I can—

He pulls out, flips me over and covers me with his mouth. I'm dripping wet with his come and my own wetness, and I still want more. I ride his face and it's fast and brutal. He pushes me toward my orgasm ruthlessly, tonguing and kissing and sucking me. I come apart in seconds, crying out and squeezing his head between my thighs.

"Harper."

He says my name, and I'd like to think I hear other things in that one word. Things like *I'm sorry* and *stay* and *be mine*. But this is dirty hookup sex, not a box of candy hearts. I don't get my choice of sweet messages. I don't get his heart.

My dress is still up around my waist, and I've completely lost my panties. And my mind.

"This isn't a booty call," I whisper into the sheets. Then I say it again, louder, with different words. "This matters. We matter."

He looks at me and time slows down. I want to grab his shoulders and shake him. Kick him hard in the balls because maybe then he'll finally feel something for me. It's so stupid, wanting more from a man who's told me over and over that he can't. That he *won't*.

"I love you," I say and wait.

There's a long, painful moment of radio silence. I roll onto my side, and he lets me go.

"Fuck, Harper," he says finally.

That is so not an *I love you, too*.

His hand comes up, like maybe he's about to brush the hair back from my face, but I bare my teeth at him and he backs away before I bite his finger the fuck off. It's obvious that *can't* and *won't* mean *don't* and *never fucking ever.* So it makes no sense for me to stick around. To stick with him. He's not in love with me.

    I get up.

    I get dressed.

    And then I leave.

CHAPTER TWENTY-ONE

Vik

WHAT'S WRONG WITH straight-up sex?

Harper's been my dirty girl, my fun girl, my one-night stand on fucking repeat.

Gotta love that.

I've never gone for seconds or thirds. I get around, but when I'm in your bed, I make sure you have a damned good time. Harper just got a little more of me than normal. Nothing wrong with that. No promises, no strings, no meaning. I don't know where she's got this idea that we should be something else. Why fuck with a good thing? Why risk screwing it up?

I think about this off and on for the next week. It's hard. Or maybe that's because after Harper walks out on me, things take on a fuzzy, dazed quality. Isn't that what all those stupid songwriters claim? That they're walking through rainstorms, fog storms, totally apocalyptic storms?

I just sort of want to see Harper again.

A lot.

I ink giggling college freshmen and have no one to tell. I catch myself drawing pictures to capture moments that will make Harper smile, but there's no place to send them.

She's just...gone.

And having just lost my dad, I've got more experience than I'd like with absences. I'd like to believe that someday, on some road, some place, my dad and I will ride together again. Problem is, that's not today and it's sure as fuck not tomorrow. I don't have a choice about that timeline and I'll have to wait, but with Harper?

I kicked her out.

I told her to go, and she did.

That makes this absence my fault. And when it's your fault, you can't just change your mind and, boom, you get the missing person back. But I wish I could. I wish she were right here, in my arms, and we were fighting or loving, laughing, living, inking— doing anything and everything instead of nothing.

CHAPTER TWENTY-TWO

Vik

TO WIN HARPER BACK, I need a plan. A really awesome, kick-ass plan. After all, Harper's almost as in love with her planner as she used to be with me. She loves forethought, organization and ten-step strategies for handling anything and everything. If I want to show her that I've changed and convince her that I love her, it's not enough to drop at her feet and start belting out the *I love you*s. I wouldn't believe me, either.

I'd insist on proof.

Lots and lots of fucking amazing proof that did *not* involve our bodies getting naked and exchanging dirty favors—although I'm totally making a list for our honeymoon. Yes, *honeymoon*. I'm dreaming big. And anyhow, the longer I have to fantasize, the more creative I'll be. It'll be like my really early, super-awesome Christmas present to her.

Huh. Now, that's an idea. I could make Christmas come early. Never mind that it's September, we live in Vegas and we have more palm trees than

pines. My planning ahead should just score me bonus
points. I whip out my phone and Google-fu nets me
the seeds of a plan. You know that song "Twelve Days
of Christmas"? If you don't, you're about to.

I kick off Monday by sending a prospect to Harper's
work with an early Christmas present. I'd bring it myself, but she's currently pissed off and not answering my
texts. Pretty sure I'll get shit from the rest of the club
about my presentation, but I'll deal. Goolie certainly
isn't happy about the big, pink box he gets to carry on
his bike. Or maybe it's the even larger black velvet ribbon that took me fucking forever to tie. FYI, there are
much better ways to spend an hour with ribbon. I'm
hoping Harper keeps it and I can show her.

Inside the box is a planner. It's pink to match the
box, and I nearly gave myself second-degree burns
hot-gluing the black bows to the front. From the number of bow-bedazzled clothes in Harper's closet, I've
deduced she *really* likes bows—so I'll give them to
her. The inside of the planner, however, reflects my
tastes. I've cut-and-pasted pages from the *Kama
Sutra*. We can pick a different position for each day
of the year.

Harper doesn't say anything.

No texts.

No phone call.

No fucking skywriter drawing my name and hers
across the Vegas sky.

Sure, that last one's a stretch, but I won't think
about failing. Losing Harper isn't an option. Since I
have a bike and know where she is, I ride over at five

o'clock to wait in the parking garage next to her car. Five o'clock becomes six and then seven. It's ridiculous how much she works. When she finally appears, it's almost eight and she looks exhausted. She also looks good enough to eat. Her pink shirt's got a bow sitting right over her tits and her heart, just pointing the way for me.

She doesn't see me because she's so intent on reaching for her door handle. Her face is strained, and she has the look of someone getting the hell out of dodge. She juggles an impressive mountain of paperwork as she points her clicker at her car. It's definitely intervention time.

"Babe. How was your day?"

She shrieks, paper mountain collapsing in an avalanche, and she points the clicker at me. Thank fuck it's not a gun or I'd be a dead man.

"You." Her eyes narrow.

"Me." I consider going in for a hello kiss, but her eyes promise that would just seal my death sentence. I settle for crouching at her feet and scooping up her papers. Gives me a real nice view of her legs, too.

"What is this?" She smacks me on the head with her new planner. She makes no move to help me in my collection attempts. That's okay—I've got no problem sitting at her feet for hours. Might eventually have to work my way up—with my mouth—but I'm a patient man. Mostly.

"It's a Christmas present," I tell her.

"It's September." The tone of her voice seriously questions my sanity.

"Christmas is coming early this year. That's your first present."

"There are more?" She sounds distinctly *un*thrilled.

I hum a few bars of the "Twelve Days" song and she groans.

"Are you here to torture me?"

"Nope."

"Then what are you doing here?"

"Giving you a heads-up." I grab the last paper, pat the mess into a vaguely rectangular shape and stand up. "I'm giving you the twelve days of Christmas and tomorrow's our first day."

"I don't want Christmas. I don't want twelve days with you. And there's no *us*." She stabs me in the chest with the clicker after each sentence.

I open her car door, drop the stack of paper inside and then hold the door for her like a fucking gentleman. I should paint my Harley white and pretend it's a horse and I'm a knight.

"What do you want, Vik?"

I keep it short and sweet. "You."

She's equally to the point as she drops into the driver's seat. "Fuck off."

Do you know the words to the Christmas song? Because whoever wrote that thing had the world's worst taste in Christmas gifts. Asshole definitely wasn't a Macy's shopper. The first day of Christmas calls for a partridge in a pear tree. Achieving this requires a minor felony on my part and takes the better part of Tuesday. I bribe one of the Bellagio's waiters for one of those silver room service domes and then I load it up with a nice roast chicken and a poached pear swimming in something alcoholic. More money changes hands when I reach Harper's building and it gets me inside to her front door. This is where the second felony comes in.

I'm naked except for the bow around my neck. Harper really, really likes bows. And dinner. And sugar. I'm just hoping she likes me most. I lean hard on her bell because this whole plan will go much better if she spots me before her neighbors do. It's twenty-four long, naked seconds before she opens the door. I count each one, which just goes to show how much Harper's changed me, right?

"Jesus." She stares at me and I refrain from the obvious jokes about not being a deity. Instead, I wave the tray at her.

"Surprise. Can I come in?"

Look at me using my company manners and asking instead of telling.

"You're naked." She looks a little wild-eyed. Also, her gaze may dip beneath my bow. She's welcome.

"I'm apologizing," I correct. "I fucked up big-time, Harper. I get that. You told me that you loved me, and I told you shit. You want me down on my knees? Because I can do that."

"What makes you think this is what I'd want?"

"Me? On my knees? I think you'd fucking love that, babe."

Generally speaking, groveling isn't something I do. Ever. And getting down on my knees only hap-

pens when it involves pussy and my tongue. But for
Harper? Anything's possible. I drop down and set
the tray down on the floor in front of me. This both
frees up my hands and prevents her from slamming
the door closed.

"Oh my God." Her gaze darts down the hall.

"Can I come in?"

"No."

"Can I apologize?"

Christ, she's fucking beautiful. My dick picks this
grossly inappropriate moment to stand up and ap-
plaud her.

"Go." She points toward the elevator. "Just—go."

"I brought you dinner. It's a partridge and a pear.
Not sure I worked out the 'in a tree' part, but I'm hoping you cut me some slack." I nudge the room service
tray toward her, and for a minute, I think I've got her.
Then she shoots the tray back toward me, zips inside
and slams the door. I retrieve my clothes from the
stairwell, get dressed and move on to the next step
in my plan. I've got eleven more days, as I explain to
the homeless guy I end up sharing the chicken with.
We sit on the curb, picnicking, and I figure day one
could have gone worse.

The second fucking day of Christmas calls for tur-
tledoves. Since real birds shit everywhere and would
disagree with Bing's digestive tract, on Wednesday
I clean the drugstore out of Turtles and Doves. I take
the whole lot of chocolate over to Harper's office at
dark o'clock and let myself in. This requires smiling

charmingly at her assistant, who's more than willing to let me wait for Harper in Harper's office. I keep my clothes on this time because Harper loves her goddamned job and I won't do anything to jeopardize it.

"Day two, babe," I tell her when she shows up clutching a coffee. Since I'm sitting on her desk, she can't exactly miss me. Figure I won't scare the shit out of her this time, either.

She jabs a finger at the sugar mountain stacked beside me. "What is this?"

Since she asked, I sing her the verse. "On the Second day of Christmas my true love sent to me two turtle doves and a partridge in a pear tree." I pause. "I didn't bring you another chicken, though. Didn't seem like breakfast food. Guess I could have gone for chicken and waffles. You want a redo?"

She rubs her temples. "Why are you here? Why do you think I'd want you here?"

"I know what you like." The trick is to sound confident. Remember what I said before? Harper. Forgiveness. Another chance. That's all that matters.

"How do ten thousand calories reflect your greater understanding of me?"

"You like candy. You like laughing. You have an awesome fucking sense of humor."

Harper stares at me like I've lost my mind. Which I may have. My dad would have smacked me upside my head, and he'd have been right. Of course, he'd also have laughed his ass off—and then he'd have suggested that we fill Harper's office to the ceiling with candy. Go big or go home, right?

Thinking about him hurts just a little less today, although it still feels like getting a root canal with no drugs. And possibly using a shovel to do the digging around in my gums. Or my heart.

Harper braces her hip against her desk. She hums a bit of the song. "You're really doing the entire song?"

"You bet." And because I'm all in and dignity has gone out the window already, I start belting it out at the top of my lungs. I hop off the desk, grab her hands and dance her around in circles. I even throw in a few pelvis thrusts.

"Oh God. Stop." She's giggling, though. She doesn't look pissed off anymore. She looks…happy.

I stop.

"You want me to strip? I'll give you breakfast and a show."

Don't think I didn't plan for this. Thanks to the staying power of the Sharpie, I've drawn a hundred big, black, loopy bows on the Calvin Kleins I bought precisely for this occasion.

Harper slaps a hand over my mouth. "Not in my office."

"Where?"

This seems promising. Like hot-makeup-sex promising.

"You need to go." She starts shoving boxes of chocolate underneath her desk. She must have an early meeting.

"I'll go if you promise to read the plan I've put together and go over it with me tomorrow."

She pauses in her candy cleanup. "You want me to go over your plan?"

I go with the truth.

"You like plans. You like to know where things are going. So I made one for us."

Honestly? What I want is for her to go out on a date with me. Make love with me. Ride with me, fight with me, love me. It's that last part of the plan that's most important.

She stares at me.

Pretty sure she's trying to figure out the fastest way to get my ass out of her office because she comes to the obvious conclusions.

She gives in.

"Okay." She scowls. "But you have to wait until Saturday. Some of us have bosses that care if we show up."

I ignore the dig because I'm one step closer to my goal. To *Harper*.

Thursday the song calls for three French hens. In retrospect, I should have gone with "99 Bottles of Beer on the Wall." Courting would have been much simpler. Finding French hens in Vegas is every bit as difficult as you think. The only reason I don't visit a damned pet store is that Bing would either vote me off the island or have lunch. Instead of wildlife, I send a six-pack of beer from a brewery that does a Twelve Days of Christmas series. I scribble a note that's three-quarters picture, one-quarter words. The picture is me trying to tree three very reluctant hens in a palm. I think for a minute and then go with more truth. I tell her how much I want to be with her to celebrate all her milestones. And how I'll be there if she lets me for the shitty days, as well, but with an even bigger beer.

Friday I up my game and actually produce four calling birds. Okay. So she doesn't get to take them home with her, but I think she'll like this better. I adopt four black-and-white penguins at the zoo on her behalf. Since my large check comes with naming rights, I christen them Harpsichord, Harpie, Doodle and Monster Dick.

Today, however, is Saturday.

D-Day.

And either Armageddon or the second coming of Christ when I succeed or fail at convincing Harper to take me back. And yes, I'm feeling the pressure. It may have taken me way too long to realize what I feel for Harper, but now I'm hopelessly, headlong in love with her, and she's the only woman for me.

I pick her up and she settles behind me, her arms wrapped around my waist. See how we fit together? The way we move together as we ride down the Strip?

That's the best fucking sign right there.

I just need to convince Harper. When we get to the Bellagio, I pull over. I've got a buddy who owes me and I'm cashing in all my favors.

"You're going to get a parking ticket." Harper's forehead gets these cute little creases when she's trying to figure out what I'm up to.

"Watch." I switch places with her on the bike because I need to hold her.

Her frown gets deeper. "The fountain show doesn't go off for another eleven minutes, Vik."

I slide my arms around her. How can I not hold on to this woman? Not only is she fucking gorgeous, but she's the smartest person I've ever met. She's organized, funny and has a dirty streak that will make me a very happy man.

"Three," I whisper against her hair.

"You're not singing again, are you?"

She doesn't pull away, and I almost get distracted by the amazing way she smells.

"Two."

I kiss her ear just because it's there and I'm weak. Christ, I love every inch of her. Her hair's pulled back in a ponytail that begs for me to fist it.

"One." I bite down lightly because some things won't change.

She rewards me with a little moan—just as the fountains explode. Timing is everything. The water soars upward, "Twelve Days of Christmas" blaring from the hotel's speakers. While she stares slack-jawed at the show, I scoop her up and stride over to the fountains. By the time I've planted her ass on the railing and caged her in with my arms, she's coming back to her senses.

"You planned this?" She sounds dazed.

Mission fucking accomplished.

"You said I never planned anything. That I never

looked ahead. I just never had anyone I wanted to plan for."

"And now?" She licks her lips. I don't think she likes having nothing between her ass and an entire lake but me and a very thin railing. I'd like to tell you that I immediately set her back on her feet, but that would be untrue. I love having her off balance and hanging on to me. I won't ever let her fall.

"I'm hoping I've got you." I wrap my arms around her back, pulling her closer. "You're my tomorrow and my tomorrow after that. Give me a chance to prove that to you for the next sixty years or so."

"Vik?"

"Yeah, babe?"

"I forgive you. Can you let me down now?"

She *really* doesn't like her current position, does she? I take shameless advantage.

"Wrap your legs around me."

She does, and I can't stop myself from patting her ass as I twirl her around in the biggest goddamned circle. Tourists are looking at us like maybe we're an act and they should drop a quarter in our hat. Let them look. I'm holding all I need.

Well, except for one teeny tiny detail.

"Did you bring the planner I gave you?"

"Yes?" She sounds a little breathless. I slide her down my body, making sure I touch every smoking-hot inch of her.

"Take it out."

She gives me a look. I'm gonna become really familiar with that look over the coming years if I'm lucky. That look says we're in public and I just said something filthy. Still, she fishes the hot-pink planner out of her purse and hands it to me.

"Did you read my plans for us?" I drop down onto a bench. The fountain show is wrapping up, and my friend is probably getting all kinds of shit for his off-script performance. I'll make it up to him later.

Harper flushes. "I read through October. You have a filthy imagination and no one could possibly have that much sex."

I look forward to proving her wrong.

"We wouldn't work," she says, shaking her head. "I like rules and plans and sticking to one path. You may want me right now, but at some point—"

"We can argue over which direction we go or what road we take. We'll be like those old couples fighting in the parking lot, and we'll do it with love. I can be your Mr. Right. I can be whoever you need, Harper. You just gotta let me try."

I flip the planner open to the spot I've bookmarked with a hot-pink ribbon. Guys don't hot-glue-gun shit ever. Not unless they're MacGyver and they're building a nuclear reactor out of spare crap in their garage. The lady at the crafts store showed me how to do it, though. Wouldn't let her touch it because it had to come from me. Especially since there's a big-ass diamond ring hanging off the end of the ribbon.

"I love you," I say.

And then I haul my T-shirt up and show her my new ink. Pink, black and right over my heart, Harper's face is inked into my skin. The words beneath it read

Property of Harper. It's my very own property patch. You have to be strong to partner with a man who belongs to an MC. Harper's got that strength. She's always had it. But if I want her to throw in with me, I'll have to be there for her, too.

And I really fucking want to.

"You mean it?" She blinks and for a moment I think she's about to cry, but then a blinding smile breaks through, lighting up her own face. "I love you, too."

"You be mine, I'll be yours and we'll live happily fucking ever after." I gesture toward my bike. "And if that doesn't work, we can at least ride off into the sunset every night."

"Together." She sighs.

And that's it. That's my perfect answer, my second shot at happiness, my whole world, because she throws her arms around me and there's nothing better than this.

* * * * *

LET'S TALK
Romance

For exclusive extracts, competitions
and special offers, find us online: